Children of Dionysus

Always Dark Angel Series
Book One
Edition 2: 2017
Copyright © 2014 JN Moon
GrippingReadsLtd Production Ltd
Edited by Deadra Krieger
Cover art by Andrei Bat

Acknowledgements

I WOULD LIKE TO THANK my friends who have stuck by me and supported me during the highs and lows of writing this. And the family I live with who have barely seen me for months as I disappear into the writing cave when I'm not out in the world for the day job.

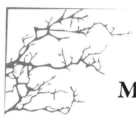

Make Contact

To receive my monthly newsletter, get awesome free stuff or be an ARC Reader just click here... alwaysdarkangel[1]
I don't spam and I never share your details
Facebook Group: Moon Council of the Supernatural: join to see cover reveals, behind the scenes and discuss all things supernatural.
https://www.facebook.com/groups/247165435816384/

---

1. https://alwaysdarkangel.com/

The Vampire

By JN Moon

ON ONE SUCH NIGHT
So full of dread
Our fate came forth
And raised his head
Terror struck
We couldn't flee
With his arms around us, he whispered
"Come with me."
We entered in a room and saw
Bones and flesh upon the floor
And stone for walls
And then did he
Sit upon what seemed his throne
It was set in stone and carved with wood
To us he gazed, then laughed so deep
And then to us, he did speak
"Drink my wine, and tell me why
Such ancient knowledge you mortals seek?"

So, there we sat by fire, warm
Sipped the wine and pondered our thoughts
That here we were with this such being
Explaining to him our thoughts and feelings.
After this talk, he gave us more wine
And then whilst smiling, gave an unearthly sigh
"I will tell you all about me"
Then with an alluring smile, he said softly to me
"And I will tell you of how I feel,
Have I compassion, love?
After all this, decide for yourselves, will you join me forever?
Or meet my maker in Hell?
But consider this wisely because there's no going back,
But if you are strong,
You'll never worry about that."
So silently we listened, we thought, we understood
And then before dawn,
We decided, we should.

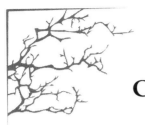

Conception

Anthony

WHAT WOULD YOU DO IF you woke up a vampire? I was just like you, the guy next door living a normal life. Until one night when my world went to Hell.

I am a predator living on human blood and I have killed both innocent and evil humans.

I've been a vampire for only one year now.

You may think this sounds exciting. Was I changed by some shadowy captivating figure from the night?

It wasn't like that. It wasn't like that at all.

It was night, cold and sheeting down rain as I walked home. The yellow glow of the streetlights reflected in puddles and the wind howled.

My soaked clothes stuck to me and the wind blew my hair relentlessly into my face like an onslaught. I hate strong wind with rain and I couldn't wait to get home. To have a hot shower, dry clothes, and something to eat.

At first, I ignored the group of vagrants at the far end of my street. They were causing the usual amount of trouble such folks do. The few people around ignored them as best they could.

After some time, I don't remember how long, I noticed I was the only person walking on my street. That's when they approached.

Their faces distorted, dark with filth and lines so deep they mimicked masked fiends. God, they stank like decaying bodies. I don't remember all the details, but I do remember it was violent, bloody, and swift. Predators taking down their prey in the blink of an eye. They were so wild, vicious, and horrifying. As they sank their razor-sharp teeth into my skin and started drinking, paralysis overcame me. I tried, but I couldn't move. I know now that their venom holds a chemical that prevents coagulation, but terrifyingly it literally paralyses their prey. Me.

I couldn't move or scream and I watched in full horror. Felt the torture. And there was nothing I could do. Fear is too less a word. Blood everywhere and the pain, agonising, causing me to sway in and out of consciousness, and the most petrifying sensation of having my blood sucked out of me.

One on my neck, one on my wrist, one on my femoral artery. They pawed at me like rabid animals, fighting over my blood. Guttural noises came from these deranged demons. I grew weaker and weaker with every second and found myself completely and utterly powerless to stop it. All I could do was watch. My veins felt taut as they strained to drain my blood.

My stomach rolled with nausea and I plunged into panic. They were merciless and I was dying. They drained me and then forced me to drink their blood. Their vile, thick, putrid blood, but my will to survive kicked in and I fed and fed and fed. As I did this I heard their laughing and they began pawing at me again. Sounds of approval, of mocking but never of speech. I think these wretches had no language of their own. Ghoulish figures of death.

Then everything went blank.

When I came around, agony raged through me. My own blood covered me and I crumpled up in horror. Huge waves of nausea overcame me and I was sick and dizzy. The world spun around me. Eventually, I managed to struggle to my flat, through the door, and collapsed. There I stayed for days.

When I awoke, I managed to get to bed and I lay there, freezing cold then boiling hot. Fever swept over me in a great surge of waves. Days had passed and a number of calls went to the answering machine. My mobile buzzed with messages, calls, and then went dead as it lost its power.

Nausea persisted and anything I previously ate had long since departed. I couldn't eat and water, only made me sick. If I drank it, I vomited it out violently. I was weak, scared, and isolated in my fear. What was happening to me? I slipped in and out of consciousness, hallucinating, the room spinning and morphing into liquid. Closing my eyes made it worse and helplessness gripped every breath.

My girlfriend Rachel was the first to know something was wrong. Fortunately for her, we were not living together, but she had a key and visited me after days of unanswered calls.

She and my close friends buzzed around me as I slipped in and out of reality. I was lucky I guess that they asked my consent before getting a doctor, which I refused in my haze. Visions of my friends admitting me to an institution for *my own good*, and being locked away in a mental asylum wearing a straitjacket if I told them what had happened, if I told them I had drunk blood. I thought I was going to die, but I clung to the hope if I could just make it through.

I kept questioning myself as to what had happened. Had it been real? But I was too afraid to tell Rachel or even my closest friends. Only the basics, a group of vagrants had mugged me. Maybe I *should* go to a hospital. I couldn't tell them I had been drained of blood, right? I definitely couldn't tell them I drank the blood of those who attacked me. As I watched them, my friends, I felt even more remote from them. Knowing that if they knew what had happened, my fate would be sealed and I would be locked away. I loved them, but this distance grew.

"Tell me what happened. I can't believe this is just from an attack. You must have caught something. Hep B? You need a doctor," Rachel and my closest friends persisted. I have a vague recollection of them standing around my bed looking scared.

"Jesus Rachel, we need to do something. He looks like Death." I heard my best mate Chris gasp.

"I know, Chris, but he refuses. I don't know what else we can do. Call his parents?"

To this, I bolted upright. "Get out now. Please leave me alone. Don't contact my family."

Immediately after this, dizziness swirled in my head and Rachel helped me lie down. She was a real angel.

They took turns staying by my bedside. I felt awful for putting this on them, but however much I protested, they would not leave. The chasm between us grew and my gut felt like it had a tourniquet wrapped around it. I had known Chris for years. We met as children at Kung Fu. This distance, my awareness of something happening to me, made my heart ache.

After a couple more days, my metabolism started to show the signs that it was adjusting. Little did I know back then, it really was a life and death situation. That most victims that get bled and fed don't survive. I didn't know the mortality rate was so high. Back then, I didn't know anything.

My vision increased. Previously I'd worn contact lenses, and now without them, I could see intricate details around my bedroom. My hearing also amplified. I could hear my girlfriend and my friends whispering about me in the living room.

Now they were scared for a different reason. Their fear had changed. They no longer feared me dying; they could see I was recovering.

What they didn't realise was what they were feeling is the same fear prey animals live by. The fear of their death. They sensed some predatory power emanating from me. Their gut instincts told them they were not safe near me, and they were right.

It was awful to see. I loved these people. They were my family.

Suddenly, my life flashed before me. Although at this stage, I didn't know what I was, I had the deep suspicion that I would no longer grow old with these people. I sensed a growing strength within my body and dangerous, violent impulses raced through me.

Fear crept over me; I knew I would have to leave them. I knew I wanted to hurt them. I didn't understand what I was feeling or why. What the fuck was happening to me? In my mind's eye, I had a violent urge to strike out at them and do... Do what? Maybe I was going insane after all.

My friends started to stay away after that day, but Rachel, Rachel and I were in love and love knows no bounds.

Fear held me in its grasp—a dark force pulsating through me, a power that wanted to hurt her. I *was* losing my mind, but I couldn't tell her. I was too ashamed, too afraid. I couldn't accept the way she'd look at me if I told her how I felt.

So, I tried to rein in these deep physical impulses. It was futile. What made it worse was that she was so understanding. She knew something had changed me and she tried to accommodate me, to help me. But deep down inside I was beyond her help.

"Anthony, you know I love you. What can I do?"

"Just go, I need some space," I snapped. She looked so forlorn. Only a while ago we were happy, laughing, loving, and living.

"I'll get my stuff," she sighed.

As she packed her few things up, I remembered the times we'd shared together, the silliness. When we cooked together we'd make up songs and dance around. What was this dark force within me? Gulping hard to fight back the tears I couldn't look at her.

She hesitated before kissing me goodbye. I was sprawled out on my sofa staring at the ceiling. Suddenly, her scent overwhelmed me and I could taste her. I grabbed her head as she bent over me.

"Sorry, I'm so sorry, don't go. I love you, I love you so much," I gasped. Our kiss was long and sensual; the first kiss for a long time.

I pulled her onto me and suffered such a burning desire that I became forceful, desperate, and fierce. She didn't resist and she seemed to welcome this.

On the one hand, I wanted her, wanted to love her, caress her, and make love to her. On the other, I wanted to bite her. *Bite her*? I battled with my mind. *I must be going insane.*

She grabbed me, too late to go back now. After all, if I was insane, this could be my last time I make love to a woman, my woman who loves me. I reasoned I was strong enough to overcome this darkness. I had, after all, been with Rachel for many years and I would keep her safe, wouldn't I?

She climbed off me and unzipped my jeans and as she went down on me, the sensation was nothing I had ever experienced before. It was ten times more intense than I'd ever encountered. Shivers of desire ran through my body, and my breathing slowed. I pulled her up and lay her down, and as I went to return the favour, my attention was drawn instinctively to her femoral artery on her thigh. Pulsing blood. My vampiric eyes honed in on it, the scent of blood drawing me.

What the Hell, don't think about it! I screamed in my mind. But after a few more minutes I became so drawn to it that I pulled myself up and made love with her.

There lay my next problem. As she writhed around, moaning, and tilting her head in-between kissing, I came face to face with her jugular vein. Automatic responses targeted veins, the pulsing, the scent.

This desire to bite her, to drain her was built in me, escalating like a tornado, growing stronger and stronger.

As we peaked, I yelled with relief and fear.

She must have thought this was due to all the past events, but it was shock, frustration, and anger because in the next seconds I was sucking on her femoral artery. I knew my teeth were sharp, but in all the craziness I had tried to dismiss this. I'd tried to dismiss a lot actually.

She screamed as my teeth pierced her flesh, squirming and then became quite still. Her eyes glazed, and I realised then that my bite had sedated her. By biting her, drinking her, I, too, had released a chemical that paralysed her, just as had happened to me.

Minutes later I stopped—shit it was hard! —and jumped back, blood running out my mouth and down my chin.

"You have to leave, Rachel, now," I screamed. "I'm going to hurt you. I can't control it."

Still, she lay there dazed, peaceful, looking almost dead.

Upset I grabbed her clothes and shook her. Slowly she started to come around. "Rachel, please get out, this is too much," I said frantically, helping her get up.

"Anthony?" her eyes glazed. "You died?" she whispered. Then she dressed without another word or glance and left.

I threw myself onto my sofa and wept, impulsively licking the blood from my hands and lips which made me feel worse. The compulsion of wanting more blood repulsed me. I repulsed myself. More blood, I needed more. Turbulent cravings consumed my mind, my body. My body raged for it. And shock—shock at what I had just done.

I turned the lights off, paced up and down, and punched my fist through the wall. Astonishing myself at my strength, I sat down, got up, and allowed my mind to roar in all its fury as my heart pounded and raced with Rachel's blood flowing fast through it. Through me.

My future loomed before me like a dark ocean, wild and powerful. I was Godforsaken and cut off from my friends and family. I started laughing crazily. *I must be insane. Is this what insanity is like?*

Despair and loneliness consumed me.

After that, I didn't go out for some time and I didn't see anybody.

My doom emerged in front of me as I saw my future as a madman who believed he needed human blood—his girlfriend's blood. Everything was dark. She was right. I had died inside. I realised that when I drank her blood elation had filled my every bone, every part of my body had felt alive, powerful, not sick, as I would have expected. The sweet taste upon my lips fixated me so instinctively; I licked them at the thought of it. My mind and body, even my soul seemed engrossed on her blood. That was chilling.

All I knew was that I was faster, craved human blood, and I now looked at people as food.

A surreal nightmare, and finally the hunger got to me. I decided to go out, the blood driving me until I couldn't bear it any longer.

So, I did, not knowing what would happen.

Would I kill? Would I terrorise some human and drink them? I dreaded my future, I dreaded myself. Finally, I let go and embraced my nature, the core that was me. I surrendered to it.

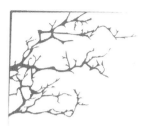

First Kill

Anthony

THAT FIRST KILL WAS bloody, violent, and filled me with fear. Fear of myself. What the hell had happened to me?

My victim was a woman who I met at a bar. Vivacious and intelligent, the sort of woman I would willingly date. She eyed my untouched drink with suspicion but was too enamoured by my ethereal charms to consider her danger. Ah, part of our weaponry to entice you in.

Sweeping my hair out of my face, I held her gaze too long to be polite. Closing the gap of personal space, I breathed her in, she moved unsteadily as she seemed hypnotized.

"Your eyes, so deep," and reaching out she impulsively touched my face, her hand lingering on my cheek. She was spellbound and I, I was hungry.

I suggested we go to another bar which, of course, I had no intention of doing.

As we walked in the rain that night laughing and flirting, I wanted her and I wanted her blood. She would be my first. I hated myself at that moment. Thoughts of suicide permeated my mind. But the blood, her blood...my whole body ached for it.

I gently pulled her into me; I could taste her scent, intoxicating me. Brushing my lips on her face, and pressing my lips to hers, she tasted sweet like the wine. Taking her hand, gazing into her eyes, I led her down a back street and kissed her fervently.

She was mesmerised into my presence and after more kissing, I started to undo her shirt. Her body was voluptuous and firm. She pulled me into her, tighter.

She was captivated and I took her up against the wall, amazed at the ferocity of my own strength.

Her porcelain skin appeared so smooth, and I greedily wanted so many sensations at once. Her blood swarming through me. Reaching nirvana.

I felt ravenous, crazed, totally obsessed. Doomed.

But it was neither swift nor smooth.

I fumbled and bit, not a clean bite, and she gasped in pain and shock.

She swooned and I had to hold her upright, pushing her back against the wall, the craving raged in my body whilst she struggled and I kept biting, snapping, tearing, and then held her fast in my grip.

She tried to scream in sudden horror. I will never forget that look, so swift from Paradise to Hell in a second. I placed my hand roughly over her mouth and said, "Shhh, easy now. I will have you," in a soft voice.

She tried to scream through my grip and struggled, but I tightened my hold and finally, finally, I began to drink her blood. Then she was paralysed. I knew she would be completely conscious, but unable to move. Only to watch and feel me as I sucked on her soft neck. Her eyes glazed.

I don't know why but the moment before she died, I stopped drinking and looked her in the eye. Saw her staring back at me. Her eyes filled with abject terror and hate.

Maybe I thought I owed her that at least, the guts to look her in the eye whilst I stole her virtue, her trust, her life. Then I was drinking again like a frenzied demon. I didn't stop. I could feel her life fading away from her until I had drained her dry, her heart slowing, and then I pulled away abruptly and she slumped against the ground.

In that second, she became abhorrent to me. I can't explain. But her dead body repulsed me, my first blood.

I could still smell her on me and my body ached. Her scent surrounded me. I could still feel her and the growing anguish of wanting more, more blood, more sex.

I left her there and ran and ran. My legs seemed to glide with speed, almost flying through the streets and out of the city. I ran to the park, dawn now a few hours away, and sat with my head in my hands and my soul in hell.

I couldn't live like this. Was I really a vampire now? Had I lost my mind, my soul? But my soulless body and my soulless mind wanted more blood, more sex and it raged inside me like an unstoppable terrifying monster.

I wept. Salty tears mixed with precious blood ran down my face and stung my cheeks. I rocked back and forth at the sheer horror and power that I now wielded.

A month ago, I was living a normal life. I had a girlfriend until I ate her. I'd had friends, family, and fun. I had love, without wanting to drink all the blood in my girlfriend's body.

Now I have this. Immortal fear flooded through me, and the feeling of complete and total isolation from everyone and everything. Still, the hunger was intense, sweeping in waves, growing stronger and stronger.

I want to drink you, I want to feast on you, I want your blood.

I am a dark angel. I will draw you in, take you. And then I shall drink your blood. All your blood.

I will discard you just as you discard your trash. In time my conscience will weaken and you will mean nothing to me.

Nothing more than sex and blood. You will die. Yet I live on, evil and debauched. Unstoppable.

Finally, I knew that I had to do something with the body.

I ran back, grabbed the vile corpse, and took it to a building site just outside the city.

It was gone, forgotten in under an hour.

And I had just over an hour to see what the world would offer me next.

Requiem for Nathaniel

Anthony

AND THEN NATHANIEL found me. Young when he was turned, Nathaniel is tall, eloquent, and very beautiful.

He must have been about eighteen years old when he was made vampire, and as such still had the look of innocence and youth in his beautiful, big brown eyes. But he was ruthless to be sure.

He approached me silently, creeping up on me from behind and stood as still as a statue watching me. I flashed around trying to grab him by the neck, then he let out the most raucous laugh that I ever heard.

"Anthony, your first night out, I take it?"

I was so shocked that I just stood there, looking at him dumbfounded.

"Ah, I see the answer is yes," he said in his elegant voice. "Allow me if you will, there's a party not far. Let's have some fun. I can see you're still in the throes of bloodlust. It's always more rampant in the beginning." His wide grin and eyes pierced with amusement conveyed an excitement over my existing state.

"Am I always to feel like this? I hate myself. I've killed and I want to kill. Help me," I blurted out like a crazed man.

Nathaniel walked slowly and purposefully up to me and threw his arm around my shoulder whilst guiding me towards the street. He whispered closely to my ear, I could feel his breath on my face, sweet and warm. "Please, Anthony, relax. I shall, if you permit me to, be your guide, your companion. You are not alone my friend, nor do I think you will ever be alone unless you choose it. You have a most incredible face, not unlike Renaissance sculpture!" he grinned.

But I was alone. Isolated from my human companions. They had been my family. I was an outsider in a strange land except I was home. This made my stomach feel like stone and my spirits heavy. Yet the hunger, the lust filled every cell of my being.

In one of the houses not far there was indeed a party. I realised that if I stole my mind away from my impending doom, I could hear and see so much. Birds rustling in the trees, the wind gently blowing, and the presence of humans. Many humans. Heady and intoxicated, I could smell them and hear them even at a distance.

As we strode in it was pitiful really. There were copious drunk and stoned people, looking the worse for wear, and then there was us. We looked like gods walking among the mortals. It was like shooting fish in a barrel.

"We'll take this one I think," Nathaniel whispered, "And that one. You see, Anthony, men, women, human, vampire; you'll find your tastes...diversify. It's different for Us. We are no longer bound by human...constraints." His last word made him smile mischievously.

"Their sexuality is irrelevant. If they are human they will be attracted to us, make no mistake. They will, of course, fear us unless they have known us prior to being turned. This will be subconscious. But ultimately, we draw them in. And they will want us. You can doubt this all you will, but it is a truth," he whispered.

"This is our sin and in time you will not care whether they are male or female, only beautiful, interesting, and good to drink."

We led the woman and the man into the back garden. As I knew what would follow the hunger became even more insatiable. It pounded in my veins and body. I was so aroused that I thought I would burst.

The alcohol had lowered the woman's inhibitions and she started to undress whilst I kissed her. I started to grab her lustfully and took her quickly. Nathaniel placed his hand on my shoulder and whispered in my ear, "Slowly Anthony, take your time. Make the experience last. It should be sensuous, dreamy, and passionate. And don't kill her," he said, after which he grinned.

But I just couldn't do that, I needed my fix and I needed it fast. My head swooned from the intensity of the sensations.

I think Nathaniel did try not to kill, not so much his conscience but rather he pitied humans, such easy prey. Even to me, his voice was hypnotic and I found myself spellbound in his presence.

But slow wasn't an option for me at that moment, and before I could drink her, I experienced the release a thousand times over.

Freedom filled my core. I forgot everything that I am. I was ripping the life from the jaws of death itself.

Nathaniel moved in front of me and spoke softly to the woman. "What's your name?"

"Faye," she replied, completely mesmerised by our presence.

"Ah, Faye." He stepped up to her kissing her softly.

The guy seeing this moved up to me. I was shocked but too hungry to care, and actually slightly intrigued.

I embraced him and kissed him, allowing his passion to enwrap me. It was weird but I wanted his blood. Nothing more. And I would do anything for it. *It* controlled me.

I moved onto his neck, amazed at how easily I spotted his artery and my teeth targeted it this time. The blood of the previous woman still coursed through my veins, so this must have helped me.

I bit, he gulped and swayed, and within seconds he was paralysed. I wanted to stop, but I couldn't. He had that same glazed helpless look and I drank and drank. I felt terrible but ravaged. This handsome young man, so trusting in my arms and watching me. I caressed his face as I sucked on his neck like a hungry young animal suckling at its mother's breast. I gorged myself on his blood.

Nathaniel was busy with Faye, screwing and drinking her, but making it look so elegant. He was like some enchanting demon. *Maybe that is what we are, demons.*

I dropped the guy on the ground, blood running down my face, dazed and scared, excited, running my fingers through my hair, I threw my head back, adrenalin coursing and stared at Nathaniel.

He whisked around to stare right into me, dropping Faye who was now completely dead. He grinned. He rushed me, grabbed me, and pushed me against the wall. He buried his face into my neck and held me close and inhaled my scent. "Exquisite," he murmured.

He pressed his body so close to mine, I could feel him against me and he brushed his lips over my face and stared longingly into my eyes. He said nothing, just held me tight and stared.

Finally, he shuddered and after a deep breath took my head in his hands, his face right up to mine. "Anthony, I've been empty but you, you give me hope. Come, dawn is approaching and I want to leave this place." He grabbed my hand and led me to his home.

I was a lost child out of its depth. Evil and yet so scared. But with the blood, their blood, my conscience was bypassed. Only the sensation of life buzzed through me like electricity pouring through me at fifty thousand watts.

So, I let him lead me where he would, not knowing what roller-coaster I would end up on next. I couldn't think, it was too awful to comprehend. I didn't want this, I didn't want any of this and the feeling of being trapped inside some violent nightmare weighed down upon my soul.

Day Walker

Anthony

NATHANIEL TOOK ME OUT the next day. I had not been outside in the daylight since the horror of the change. With my senses now so damn acute I found it too much to bear.

If you can, imagine when I'm out at night, I can hear everything. The birds in the trees, small mammals scurrying around, and owls calling, their sound like banshees from Hell to me, so damn loud. Therefore, to be out during the day in the crowds, it's akin to being in the middle of a festival with a really bad hangover and hearing everything. It's an assault on the senses.

As we are more photosensitive, I had to use sunscreen so I followed Nathaniel's advice. And sunglasses. Sunglasses are a must, but, to be honest, I am a little vain and I love style so sunglasses are easy. However, I used a pair of his. Nathaniel has impeccable taste and judging from his home, a lot of money.

"Anthony, you need to get used to being out during the day. What are you doing for money?"

"I had some saved, but I haven't worked since. I ran my own business, but now I have no idea. Everything's too much." I turned to run, to get back to his home, my breathing tight

24

and tortured in the blazing light of sensations, of noises, but he grabbed me and held me firmly by the arms.

"Look at me," he commanded. "Look...at....me.... That's right, breathe. I know, I know, it's all so noisy, so bright. Come, let us walk slowly and closely. Now focus your attention on your breathing, and try not to think much."

That made me laugh. It was like when I was studying martial arts and I would focus on my breathing and not think. He was right; this helped and I started to feel calmer.

It felt strange looking at people rushing, laughing, or miserable faces. Like ants scurrying around with absolutely no idea of our existence. Totally absorbed in their consumerism. Their narcissistic and capitalist world. We might get the odd glance from a more alert human drawn to our otherworldly charms, but no more than that.

After a while with Nathaniel close to me, I started to relax but I was ever aware of my overpowering urge to just grab someone and drain them. Or screw them. Or both.

"How the hell do we fight it, Nathaniel?"

"Practise and patience. Think of it like tantra. You're waiting for the sensation. Let the wait take you, flow with it, breathe with it, smile with it. You could have anyone, anyone at all. However, you will wait until dark when you can hunt in safety. The night is, after all, our friend, Anthony, our companion. Then you can take anyone you choose."

When people came close to me, I inhaled their exhilarating human scent and it almost sent me spinning, light headed. I started to enjoy this and now I wanted more. I wanted to interact with someone. Like mortals do. Like I used to do.

"Can we go for coffee?"

He looked at me long and bewilderingly. "You must know already you can no longer drink or eat human food and drinks?" he said, obviously shocked at my request.

I nodded that I knew this. Unfortunately, when I had tried this previously the results had not been pleasant, to say the least. I had then resolved to give up trying.

"So, for the familiarity then?" Nathaniel asked.

"That's exactly it. I want to hold a cup of fresh coffee, smell it, talk to you," I said excitedly. Panic gripped me, fighting back the waves of nostalgia for my human life.

I was desperate to cling to anything resembling normality, the ordinariness that had been my life for the last thirty-eight years. I needed something familiar, yet...

Nathaniel sensed my unease and blurted out, "Anthony, let us do it. You do need to move on and it will be tough, but in the long term, this will do no harm. You are very young in our world, you cannot blame your nature, and neither can you fight it. You were, no doubt, turned against your will. The quicker you accept this, the better. There are other ways."

Suddenly I was excited. Something shifted inside me, something I hadn't felt for so long it seemed. "Other ways? Drinking animal blood or using blood banks?"

"Oh, Anthony!" Nathaniel roared. "No. Come, let us have coffee and act as if we are two dumb humans living a nine-to-five reality, and before we hunt tonight I will introduce you to two of my good friends, Tom and Josephine. They will show you. I think you'll like them."

A mixture of emotions raced through me as I sat outside on the street terrace with my favourite coffee steaming in its mug.

I smelt it; I could identify all the ingredients now. If anything, the smell was too strong for me.

I gazed at Nathaniel, who eyed me like that of a protective older brother, but I suspected with filthier thoughts. And I thought about the possibilities of what he had said.

"Other ways…" If not animal blood or a blood bank, then what? But I knew he wouldn't tell me now. I would have to wait.

For the first time in so long, I started to feel hopeful, even with my raging desire thrashing inside me.

Here we are, two strangers locked in our dark world of violence, sex, and blood. Empty and alone, pretending to be human with only our memories of human familiarity between us. Of the lives we once had. This is what binds us, our loss. Our emptiness.

My hope of another way to coexist and my memories, they are as precious to me as the rarest diamond, and I keep them in my heart. And I had Nathaniel to keep me going.

Maybe…

Deadly Liaisons

Anthony

THE FIRST TIME I MET Tom and Josephine was memorable, to say the least.

Tom was reading Dracula, no less, in the kitchen, his feet up on the table, engrossed in his book. He didn't look up whilst we walked past.

His dark, shoulder-length hair, and goatee made him appear quite bohemian. A glass of what looked like red wine rested on the table next to him. But as he sipped it without taking his eyes from his book, I could smell it was blood.

Josephine, a porcelain beauty with long curly hair, fed on a woman's neck in the living room. The scantily dressed woman draped over the sofa, moaned as Josephine sucked on her. Intriguingly, the woman was conscious. I quickly sensed that she, too, was a vampire.

I could not move or take my eyes off them.

Nathaniel curled his lips up, his eyes twinkling as he spoke, "Anthony, this is Josephine"

Josephine cast her eyes over me looking at me sideways, not moving from her gorging, and raised her eyebrows in friendly acknowledgement. Blood was smeared around her mouth and dappled over her face.

"Hey," I called to her.

The other vampire ignored us, too enwrapped in her ecstasy to care.

"So, we can drink vampire blood?" I managed to get out, still engrossed.

"Ah, Anthony, I would willingly share mine with you, if you'd like to try."

I didn't answer him. I just kept staring at the women. The might of lust rose in me like waves in a storm, heavy and impending.

"So then, this is Tom," he said leading me away by my arm.

"Good evening, Anthony." As Tom stood up, finally putting his book down, I saw just how imposing and striking he was. He was six feet, naturally toned and muscular, and his black clothes hugged his stalwart figure. I wondered then, were all these people chosen to be vampires because of their striking looks, or maybe their looks improved with age? Was it all that blood?

His eyes were kind and deep—an old soul. He held out his hand. I shook it and his grip was firm and gracious.

"So, Anthony, welcome. Nathaniel said you wanted to know another way?"

Although Tom was amiable and welcoming, there was something about his presence. Something stilted I couldn't put my finger on. I wondered how long he had been like this, whether the hunger lessens with time. Maybe immortality stretches out before you like a vast empty abyss. Knowing that you will just go on and on, and sensations become the same and so lessen with time.

"Anthony, are you ok?" Tom seemed amused at my vacant response.

"Sorry, yes. I do want to know another way. I don't want to kill, but I have no control. But...I was thinking. I was wondering...immortality...suddenly it feels so bleak, so endless."

Nathaniel and Tom flashed a glance at each other. An unmistakable look of understanding of knowing what I had just said, and then they smiled a small grin.

"You have some insight to see all this so early," Tom said quietly. "Nathaniel, you always find the most interesting and striking vampires. You really do have a knack."

"Anthony," Nathaniel said, talking close to my face. "Most don't realise this for decades." And looking at Tom as if for support, he continued, "They're just content with screwing and killing. Leaving a trail of death and destruction. So much so in fact..." He hesitated, his brows knitted. "So much so that we are now being hunted."

Nathaniel walked over to the table and gulped down the remaining blood from the glass. He gave a sigh of delight and licked his lips.

Before I could speak, Tom uttered, "We do know who is behind this. Oh, it's not humans if that's what you think. The paranormal world is bigger than you think, Anthony. There is much, much more out there." He gestured to the window. "But we can teach you not to kill. We can show you new erotic delights, and show you the best...people to feed on. These people will give you no concern for their well-being. For they deserve no concern, and frankly we are doing human society a service."

Then Tom asked me, "So, you've never fed on vampire blood, huh?"

And with that last sentence, the conversation felt lighter.

"Uh, no. No, I haven't."

So here I am, one year on. The first month was the hardest. I had felt so alone before I met Nathaniel. Filled with rage but the loneliness, the loneliness was palpable. It made me feel malicious. Even with my new-found friends, emptiness grew inside me. I missed my human family, my Rachel, my friends. I couldn't be with them, aside from the fact that I may hurt them. Uncontrollably, they had recoiled in my presence, sensing on a deep level my dark power. And so they should. But that fact, that knowing made me angry that my life had been stolen.

I toyed with my victims, played with them, fed on them. They suffered because of my anger. They were the lowest of the low, and I took pleasure in inflicting suffering on them as they had on their victims. I left them a shell of the former person they once were, unable to communicate properly, unable to cause harm to another living being, barely functioning at all. This was my sole pleasure. And it left me hollow.

I met a few vampires. That's the funny thing; as a vampire, I started to notice other vampires whilst before I would never have known. Most of them are truly solitary, suspicious, and quite vicious.

Josephine and Tom are two vampires that became my friends, although vampire friendships are not quite the same as human friendships. Never cross a vampire. And trust? Well, trust is not something that vampires find easy.

They taught me how to hunt, about only taking if possible from evil people. Many young vampires follow this whilst our conscience allows. Evidently the older you get and maybe after seeing all your loved ones and family die of old age, your conscience matters less. Maybe it's the isolation from society?

I don't know where Nathaniel went. He said he had to leave for a while and that he regretted leaving me. I missed him. I knew his thoughts for me were based on desire.

Anything more I didn't know and as such, mine for him were not. But he was familiar to me. I felt safer with him. Kindred spirits joined in darkness.

As for Josephine and Tom, we met up nightly. They helped me maintain the necessities like keeping my flat, having money. I couldn't easily pop into work. Although I had my own business, I had to contact others to manage this, in case I accidentally drain someone. The realisation of that thought alone kept me away from those I cared for. They also taught me about the Elite, and the research that they had heard about.

The Elite were the self-proclaimed vampire nobility who were apparently researching vampires. Specifically, what pinpoints the changes in the genetics that alter a human from that of a vampire. There were stories about how the Elite were testing this on the lower order of vampires. Altering their genes, testing to get rid of the vampire disease on those they deem unworthy of immortality.

I thought this sounded great. I could, in theory, become human again. But their stories are the dire consequences of this genetic tampering on the lower legions of vampires, making them neither vampire nor human but something in-between. Unable to feed on blood or food, most die slowly of starvation whilst they go insane. And here the urban myths thrive. We have to be alert if it's true. Death is slow, agonising, and torturous. But it sounded like fantasy, conspiracy theory run wild. Vampires have a taste for drama, too, it seems.

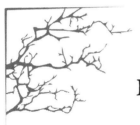

Enchanted

Anthony

JOSEPHINE LOOKED STUNNING. Her long, curly hair amplified her iridescent skin. Her outfit; how did she do it? So sexy yet so modest, her black dress fitted and flaring out to her knees. She was a bit of a closet Goth so always added a twist, her knee-length lace-up boots giving her an edge. Of course, she was the *bait* for our nightly discourse, and she knew how to work her figure.

Tom and I also made an effort. Being a vampire, one feels compelled to live up to the image, and we so enjoy the hunt that dressing up seems very appropriate. Tom often wears a hat, and always has a sense of dashing elegance about him. Although he looks a bit scruffy, he is immaculate in his grooming. Except for his hair which is shoulder length and quite messy. His scruffy style designed to look effortless.

I wore black jeans, boots, and my faithful reefer jacket with a black shirt. I often wear very cool shades, even at night because I can see so well with them, my vampire vision being so heightened. But mainly because yes, it looks cool.

We mainly hunted in Bath's Royal Victoria Park and as it sounds, a grand park full of Neo-classical statues. On entering the park, there is a large stone gateway. On top of each pillar stands life-sized stone lions, majestic and beautiful. It dates back to a time of opulence and splendour.

Where we hunt is not far from this side entrance, on a green surrounded behind by trees and flowers. In front of the green, in the distance, stands the most lavish Georgian terraced buildings set in a crescent shape. Another wonder of the city which grabbed at my fascination more, now that I was a vampire.

For us, with views of the Royal Crescent behind us, amongst the trees of the park, we felt like the actors who perform Shakespeare there during the summer months. This was our stage, with the Royal Crescent our backdrop and the green, our stage. However, our tale was much darker, more sinister, and fatal. Trembling, excitement ran through me in anticipation.

Josephine acted demurely walking through the park. How could a villain not be enticed to her?

She was enchanting and it was not long before she attracted the attention of a would-be rapist. She played them. She played them all. A look of fear on her face, of panic and the trap was set. As the villain took hold of her and she allowed him a few seconds to believe, well, whatever it was he wanted to believe.

Then she struck. Her face contorted, revealing her fangs. With vampires, expressions are everything and exaggerated. Trembling violently, his face now ashen, she grabbed him by the neck and lifted him up in all her glorious rage, as she held him there, locking eyes, and snarling.

We stole the moment where he spotted her fangs and caught his smell of sweat as shock and fear embraced him.

Slowly lowering him to the ground her grip firm - there would be no enchantment for this hapless victim, just pure terror. Tilting his head to the side, she bit into his jugular.

Tom and I sprung in like lions ready for the kill. We each drank from his wrists. It was spectacular. Crucifixion by vampires, his arms outstretched as we drank and drank and drank. Under the dark silhouettes of the trees and the slip of the moon, with the grandeur of the Royal Crescent behind us like a theatrical backdrop. We didn't stop; not that night.

We knew it was forbidden, but immortality holds no bounds and sometimes we needed the fear of breaking the rules. We hadn't even buried the body when the bloodlust took over. It was the first time I experienced such an intense bloodlust, that somewhere the lines blurred between my own sexuality. Passion and blood raged inside me, Josephine grabbed me, spun me around and thrust me against a tree, our hearts pounding fast and both of us trembling. Her scent filled my being. Intoxicating me. I had never had a vampire before and it was so extreme. I felt animalistic, powerful, and ardent. She was passionate, strong, and forceful. She pulled me into her again and again.

Tom came up behind me and started to run his fingers through my hair, kissing and caressing me, all three of us bloody, violent, and sexual. The taste of blood flowing from her mouth into mine was so hedonistic, barbaric, ecstasy. It was so wrong, which was what made it so exciting, so captivating.

I thought my head would explode any second. I'll never remember everything fully in that passionate frenzy. I was too indulged, too absorbed, so wild, so uninhibited.

Blood. We are everybody and nobody once it is in our veins.

Eventually, we found ourselves and sat under the tree satiated from blood, sex, and murder. We slumped against one another laughing, still mesmerised. At that moment, I felt invincible. They made me feel so alive, so sensual, and so out of control.

In my heightened haze, I wondered if this was why Tom and Josephine had chosen me. Had they done this before? I thought so, but what happened to the previous third party? One thing was certain; we wouldn't be making another kill that night.

But then I didn't care. My body ached in pleasure and I didn't have a care in the world, and I suffered no conscience for the victim. Not then at least.

That was the first of many nights where I found my sexuality blurred, twisted, and full of bloodlust and brutality.

I am different; my world looks, feels, smells, and tastes different.

This started to be a regular occurrence. We would lure our prey, feed in terrifying glory, and satiate our every desire. We were ever more uncompromising, both with our prey and with ourselves.

After a while, we decided we needed a change of location for our nightly impiety, so we started hitting the nightclubs where we could pick up potential victims. It became the norm for us to pick up a man and a woman, all three of us sharing their blood. We sedated them with our kiss of blood and involved them in our debauched acts of sexual hedonism.

Sometimes I would drink them all, other times just the women. It was simple; men and women were all drawn to us. Just as Nathaniel had said.

We didn't always intend to be aggressive. We're so strong, and the blood excited us to the extent where we lost the ability to act with much restraint.

For our pleasure, we exercised no control, but to follow our every whim, every desire in our true nature of vampires. In turn, we became more ruthless, more lost and without any hope of future salvation.

If I had only realised how completely remorseful I would become. How many innocent people would fall victim to our debauched terror. Well, maybe I was in too deep to stop. Like a junkie, looking for his next fix, I wanted more and more people. To drink their blood and act out every wicked fantasy my twisted mind could conjure up. I had not known my mind could be so corrupt. Maybe that darkness lives in each of us, waiting for its chance to erupt into our existence.

We—I was out of control and attracting the attention of the worst kind.

The people? Well, as I said we paralysed them with our esoteric venom. We did not always kill them and to our credit, we tried to only pick those with evil minds. However, the temptation to take and have those of a moral disposition was too great, sometimes. Just as Nathaniel had said—striking, interesting, alluring.

The ones who survived were no doubt left traumatised. Sometimes we did our best to help them, even take them home.

They had no complete recollection of what had occurred, but flashes of insight of what had happened to them. They always wanted sex, after all, they could not resist us, but the nature of it and that of the blood drinking, well, that was ours for the taking. Which was how we justified it.

In clubs, as we approached our potential victims, we felt the angry and curious stares of other vampires. It seemed that we were making a reputation for ourselves and several times during our debauched encounters, I was aware that other vampires watched us.

Yet, for a time, not one of them approached us directly. After that whilst we were out surveying our latest muse, a tall lean-built vampire called Adam approached us.

Adam wore all black, his clothes hugging his lithe figure, topped off with a jaw-dropping black military coat.

"You're all heading for disaster," he told us in no uncertain terms. "Many others are watching you. You're flying too close to the ground...and I want to join you." He flashed a smile at me.

Who were we to judge? To be honest we could not resist him.

His charm, his sculpted face with a close-cropped blonde beard, his blue-grey eyes, and straight blond hair. Beautiful. We wanted him. And he, it seemed, wanted us.

That first night with Adam was incredible. The look of wonder in his eyes, excitement, exceeding his expectations. We decided to take him back to the park; to relive our first encounters with evildoers. Josephine acted as the bait. The damsel in distress.

Adam willingly drank from the victim's wrist and he and Tom shared the blood, stopping only to pass the blood to each other from their mouths. I trembled at the ensuing lust.

He took Josephine, ripping her clothes from her like a ravaged animal, and they bit and fed on each other in the throes of desire. Blood spilled from their mouths, flowing, glistening.

Adam looked flushed and glowing, basking in the delirium of sexual hedonism and blood frenzy. And so, he stayed with us for a while.

Slowly, a few more approached us to join our debauched and fiendish games. If we wanted them, we would let them join for a while and if we didn't, we wouldn't. We were decadent, narcissistic, and ruthless.

We became blasé about it all. We chose our muses unless we went to the park to get rid of the trash that hung around there.

Sometimes, we did both. I experienced so much with so many. Treading the fine line of fear and pleasure. I was absorbed, captivated by my own rush of emotions. I didn't want it to end. But it had to.

Josephine was the first to quit. Maybe she got bored, or being around three men along with the other hangers-on was too much for her. She grew restless and dragged down by it all.

She simply left one night and Tom was beside himself. I didn't want to be without her either, but I knew deep down it was time for me to get some space.

I couldn't imagine being without Tom, and I agonised over the decision of whether or not to follow him. I made the choice and it was hard. I wanted to carry on our misdemeanours, like a boy who never wants to grow up. But I knew this wouldn't go on forever. Even as a vampire, I could not go on indefinitely. So, I chose to go it alone for a while.

Tom went off searching for Josephine, Adam hot on his tail. I would have to catch up with them later.

Endless Night

Anthony

I NEEDED TO COME UP for air. I couldn't possibly continue like the debauched creature I had become. Who the hell was I? Not Dorian Gray; that's for sure.

I'd wander around at night, still taking who-ever I wanted. It was like a new experience to me. On my own, I only felt drawn to women and I was careful not to kill them. I grew restless and a little bored with humans. They were so fragile, so predictable. Even as a human I'd never been interested in being ordinary.

There's more to life than that. Most humans I came into contact with had no spirit. No soul.

I needed another vampire, someone I didn't have to hold back with. Someone who saw the world from a different perspective. Someone to theorise with. Philosophise with. It struck me that I had been like a wild, out of control teenager on drugs, the way I acted. Vampire emotions wield so strong, like the forcefulness of nature herself.

But now, now I had time to think, to reflect. To remember who I was before this hunger infected me.

The memories of all my victims, my muses haunted me now. I'd never felt bad about taking the life of a murderer or a rapist, but I had seriously damaged innocent people, to the point where I knew they'd suffer psychological damage.

I realised with full intensity and horror that I had an eternity to dwell upon my remorseless and selfish violent nature. I wanted to curl up, to hide. The irony of it, immortal and so ashamed I wanted to die.

Was I a demon? Is that the true identity of a vampire? Is the word *vampire* just a lavish word used to describe a sick and demented demon? I could try and end this life, but I wondered if, honestly, I had the courage to do so and anyway, would it work? Maybe I would fail and become some disfigured creature. A golem wrapped in even more self-hatred, not unlike those that turned me.

I needed to figure out what I wanted to do with this life. I felt for sure I wanted to see Rachel, maybe at first just to glance at her. My heart burned when I thought that she might be dating now. Rachel with another man sent sparks of anger throughout my body, and my heart ached.

Reason and rationale told me that I had no right, no right at all to question this. After all I had done. Then I knew with absolute certainty that what we had was lost for good.

Even if she was single, I would know my recent sordid acts and I could not undo that. I had acted on base instincts, lust, blood, frenzy, and now? Now I felt cold and alone. Empty. Until my next fix.

I picked off the trash of society as I travelled. Those human wretches lurking in the dark places, playing predator. How I enjoy their retribution.

I thought of the stark contrast to my life now, as it was not so very long ago. At least I had had the sense to stay in contact with my human family by email. I told them some lies so they wouldn't question why I hadn't been to see them. I told them I was working on some international project and after the break up with Rachel, I needed to stay busy.

Rachel. How I longed for her to be in my arms once again, to smell her scent, kiss her full lips, but fear of myself prevented me from seeking her out. I did not know it then, but it would be a long time before I could see her, and even then, I wouldn't be going alone. For her safety. She was the love of my life and I missed her like I missed breathing.

I tried to block her memory, her warmth, and her affection. I craved her, yet I couldn't have her. In truth, in the darkest part of my soul, I knew that every person I had taken drove a hole into my heart. A chasm between me and my human love.

The nights were cold and bleak like my soul.

A shroud of darkness hung over me and the wind stinging my skin blew hard from the north chilling me to the core. I trawled the city every night looking for the ones who had changed me.

In my despair, I no longer cared about my appearance and the more evil people I came across, the lower my dead heart sank. I questioned this life constantly. My purpose. I could do anything now, absolutely anything. I was free. I had so few of the trappings of human society. I could ridicule these to my heart's content, but not to my soul's content.

What is in the soul of a vampire? Blood? Endurance? Am I alive now purely to exist, to fight for survival like the lion or the cheetah?

I searched the back streets of Bath, the street where I lived, and all dark alleyways I could find. But nothing. I knew that I possessed the power of many men, but the ones who turned me where in a pack. In Kung Fu, for many years I was taught to fight with various weapons, but carrying a sword or spear around the city would probably not go unnoticed. So, I chose to carry my short sticks. These are really small, but anything can be deadly when wielded with practised hands. If I met them, I would need something more than just my strength and wits. For all I knew they could be stronger.

I felt lonelier than before and decided to see if I could find Nathaniel to help me, not knowing whether or not he was back from wherever it was he went. But there was no answer from his house, and when I peered through the windows everything was immaculate, nothing touched or moved. I leant against his front door, looking for salvation. Something or someone to help me overcome this isolation and viciousness.

Was this evil always within me before I was changed? I found myself just staring down at the ground, my arms hugging my body, my mind an abyss of darkness. I was pure evil wandering the streets, arrogant in my own power and malevolence.

When I find them...

It was during this time my eyes started to open to the diversity of vampires that inhabit this planet. Even in the small city of Bath, in the dark places where no human dwells, cemeteries, crypts, and derelict buildings, vampires of the most terrifying and awful type, can be found. Similar to the ones that turned me. *The ones that turned me.* Why had they chosen me?

Maybe they had done it to mock me, an ignorant human. Such easy prey. Maybe to send my life spinning out of control and it really pissed me off that they were right. I had fallen for all the perverse antics like a moth to the flame. Yet, inside the hunger burned insatiably.

Some of the creatures I encountered were like tales of horror from a medieval age. They were very old. Some didn't speak or seem capable of communicating verbally. They were more like a rabid beast, crazed and wild. Some wore no clothes and seemed like they had no concept that they were once human unless maybe they had been born vampire and this was the result?

I shuddered to think of them and of procreating to create such vileness. Did they turn others? Were they born this way? How old could they be wandering this earth?

They meandered around silently, taking the unfortunate passer-by, drinking them dry and not caring about hiding the body. Some of them ate the bodies. It was all I could do to stop from retching as I watched in horror from a distance as these creatures devoured their prey. Demonic frenzied beings. How they escaped detection puzzled me. They were hideous. I could smell them long before I could see them. Sometimes having acute senses is not a blessing.

Their features had contorted from years of living off so few victims and they looked emaciated with their teeth exaggerated. Their eyes wide and hair dark with filth and matted. If they had clothes, these were covered in filth and it crossed my mind many times that I should end their pitiful, terrorising existence.

Others were clearly from a more recent time, and a few tried eagerly to fix themselves to me. They were sad creatures, locked in their own fear of superstitions and outdated knowledge. Their clothes were old, rotting, torn and although some of these had some remnants of their former glory in their manner, their chivalry, courtesy, and mannerisms, they were just a shadow of their former selves. Lost in the dark places, alone, frightened, and alarmed. All sense of humanity lost from them.

I had befriended such a vampire from a past age—judging by his clothes and his speech—when I came across the ones that turned me.

Immediately, as I saw them my heart raced and I found myself panting. A flashback of that night, the last night I was mortal. Anger and fear welled up in me, my muscles tense.

My body contorted and crumpled in fear, breathless from the shock and anger. Reaching for the nearest wall to steady myself, I slowed my breathing. My friend fled in that instant as I regained my sense of self.

I saw they had trapped a woman. Ironically, they were just off the centre of the city, a place I'd searched many times previously. Not far from the main high street in Bath, under the ornate pillars opposite the Roman Baths. I had to gather myself, gather my thoughts. Remind myself of my lessons from years of martial arts. Breathe.

The woman was drunk, I could see from her demeanour and scent, but she was filled with terror. Her face drained of colour, and she shook so violently with tears streaming down her face, but her voice...her voice chilled me the most. Wailing, so vulnerable, so weak. Immediately, as I assessed the situation, my own fear turned back to anger. An anger I would use calculatingly against these hateful things.

I waited for a few minutes as they toyed with her, petrifying her with slow and purposeful approaches. She panicked like a cornered animal awaiting its fate of certain death. I breathed deeply for a minute as I measured the situation and their tactics.

I climbed up the building quickly and silently just above them and then, just before they bit the terrified woman, I jumped in, yelling loudly, and whacked one of them on his temple, hard and fast. One rushed me and I kicked him full in the face, causing him to fall flat on his stinking back. The other two were writhing around hiding their faces. I jumped at the third one and front-kicked him straight in his bony chest. He grabbed my leg and I crashed to the floor.

"Run!" I yelled to the woman who was standing there startled. "Run, go!"

As the grisly creature tried to twist my leg, I pulled it in bringing him with it, closer to me, then punched his putrid face with my fist. My hand was sticky from the punch and I grimaced with disgust. Blood mixed with a vile film that hung from his flesh.

He went flying back and, as I drew breath the other two came at me and I grabbed my sticks. I stilled my mind and let my body react to the incoming attack, just as I had been trained to do. It was then I truly recognised the power not only of my changed state, but that of my Kung Fu teacher, and somewhere amid the chaos, in my mind I thanked him.

It seemed long and bloody and at last, I reacted only with instinct and not with my mind. Moving swiftly, I anticipated their moves, two of them lunged at me coming from either side. I didn't move until they were almost upon me, then I spun around, swooping low, sticks rigid in my hands smashing into the backs of their knees. As I swept up, another in my face, my fist flat I punched him fast under the chin, sending him hurtling back. Breathe. The last one, he edged from me now, growling, trying to use his inferior mind against mine. To confuse him I turned my back on him, obviously he came running. As he reached me I jumped to the side, and a whack sounded as my stick held fast in my clenched fist, I smacked into his neck, his throat. Bulging eyes, blood gurgling he cried out, shock written on his grim face as he staggered back. Surveying them, they lay there somewhere in between life and death. I questioned one of them.

"Why did you change me?" I screamed angrily into his face as the adrenalin coursed through my vampire blood. I was invincible and full of hate.

But my questions were in vain as he sniggered at me and eyed me up and down. He did not speak. Would not, or could not, I do not know. I knocked him out, punching his head into the ground. Then my rage fuelled. I kicked him in his face, his stomach. But I did not kill them. I wanted to. I don't know what held me back. My fury was burned. Maybe they couldn't be killed for all I knew.

I turned to leave that dark corner and saw the woman, their victim, crouched and shocked against the wall. As I approached her, she staggered away from me. It was time for her to pay me, my mind feeling oddly cold. I had saved her; there was a price, nothing is free. The hunger wailed at my soul after the fight, and the smell of blood awakened my being, my essence.

"It's alright, they won't harm you anymore," I spoke softly in contrast to the thoughts in my mind. "Come, let me help you home." As I led her away, she did not speak and I knew where I would lead her. Foolishly, she started to trust me as I wrapped my arms around her, comforting her and soothing her with words. An evil saviour.

That violence caused such fervour in me, as I took her in my arms and gazed into her eyes these feelings blazed in my blood and my body. Then my mind cut in, above my lust. Maybe my soul spoke to me. *Is this who I am now? You saved her. You cannot eat her. You shouldn't screw her. Take her home. And take your food from someone else.*

I wanted her so fiercely, but I didn't want to hurt her. I didn't want to leave her abused, dead like so many others. She'd been through enough. I was battling with my emotions, raw and unbounded.

It was odd to me at that moment, to act with such compassion, but I felt excited at this and almost human. Confusion compounded my mind that I wasn't going to drain her, though my body craved for her touch, her blood. I knew after all that she yearned for me, ached for me. Her eyes gazed into mine and I fought with all my will. I started to walk her home, some miles away on the outskirts of the city with my arm around her, comforting her. But then it struck me, what she had seen. And this scared me. Would she go to the authorities and tell of the wild vagrants and of the vigilante that saved her? *Well, what the fuck if she does?* I reasoned. Maybe it would be a good thing.

I walked her to her door and she turned and kissed me.

Shaking, she asked, "Won't you come in? You saved my life; I'm still scared they'll find me!"

Warmth swept over my body, as I touched her soft face and stared into her pale eyes, tired and fearful though they were. I allowed myself to hold that moment, to breathe in her scent.

Quivering, my hand brushed her skin as I placed it on her cheek and I could hear the beating of her heart pounding faster with my touch. Instinct drove me, licking my lips at the thought of tasting her.

Softly I answered, "You are quite safe now. Go. Don't invite me in!" Flashing her a smile, she gasped and stepped back.

I knew she didn't know what she was asking.

Invite a vampire into your home? Your body fills with passion, you feel on fire.

Your yearning for us is unlike any feeling you will ever have. Debauched desires awaken inside you. You cannot help yourselves.

But we, unlike you, we cannot *feel* like you. We just feed our overwhelming craving to drink you, to have your soul.

We will abuse your trust and though we can satiate your lust, satiate in a way beyond your imagining, the price is high. No coincidence that they say, *"To give yourself to a vampire is to lose your soul. Lust alone cannot sustain even the coldest of hearts. Your soul is more valuable than your life alone."*

So, I declined.

I turned on my heels and ran back to my flat. I shut the door and collapsed on my bed, the incessant hunger still gnawing at me. I wanted more and I lay there as it burned inside me. I hadn't smiled so much in a long time. I felt sensuous and dreamy even with the desire burning. I took a shower and with the hot water spraying down and that steam cleaning me, cleansing my spirit, I remembered what it was to feel worthy. Then I slept, clean, worn out, and almost at peace. I slept like the dead.

The next night I was still unsure what to do about those foul creatures. I wanted to kill them, but even after beating them, they still lived so in truth I was not sure if I could even do this. I needed to find out more about them.

I also wanted to explore my newfound humanity. I felt eager to experience these sensations of resisting desire. Desire and happiness are two separate experiences, and to be happy I needed to resist the urge to kill, to bleed. Maybe I could redeem myself if I held out longer?

Was it even possible? Tom and Josephine had promised to show me another way, and taking the blood from the evil was preferable than innocents to be sure. But then again, with them, I had been led astray. Nevertheless, I never opposed that, so I was as much to blame. I wanted very much to be better.

Since I was turned, my life had been one long, crazy, fucked up ride. No, I would search out some others who may be able to tell me more about how we came to be, and what else is out there. Just as Tom's words echoed in my mind, there is a whole other paranormal world out there. I needed a guide.

I searched out places on the outskirts of the city and came upon an underground cavern tucked away in a small, dense wood. Part of Bath is built upon mines, and it was just such a place I found.

At what looked like a rock face, a faint breeze passed me and, peering down, I saw an entrance, hidden and too perilous for humans to reach. Clambering through thick undergrowth, clinging to branches, the ledge was tiny. My footing fell away but something drove me on. Slowly I started to descend into this dark tunnel with the hope of finding something or someone to bring me peace.

As I stepped in with care, loose stones crumbled and ran under my feet. While I clung to the wall for support, a robust vampire immediately met me. Huge warm eyes scanned me followed by an even larger grin, and without speaking he pulled me down gently and led me into his lair. I felt no fear, no trepidation as there was no malice about this creature, but a warmth that was inviting.

The vampire offered me his blood. He was obviously more knowledgeable than the others were and he had created himself a sanctuary.

It was magnificent really, this underground cavern, large and regal in a medieval kind of way. Old tapestries hung from the cold stone walls, a huge roaring fire bellowed out heat in the middle of the place and as my vision followed the trail of smoke I saw an opening, a chimney that, somewhere in this wood, smoke flowed out. He seated himself on a large carved wooden chair, I was only surprised it wasn't on a dais. On either side of the fire were two low benches with old assortments of worn blankets and cloth strewn upon them. Creepily, a few skulls were placed around this little chamber, small alcoves housing them, their faces tormenting visitors in the flickering fire light.

A scattering of minions hung around, waiting on his every word. I knew he was fascinated by me ragged as I was, but to him, I was fresh, bright, and young.

His name was Sigurd, or at least that's what he called himself. He was very, very old in vampire terms, that much I could tell, though I didn't care how old he was or for his real name.

Sigurd craved the companionship of an equal. He was bored with the usual soulless creatures and the vain superficial vampires that he usually encountered. It was in his company that I realised something more profound about the nature of vampires. To become a vampire seems to draw on one's strongest traits and darkest desires, then brings these to the fore. Which might explain why when you're first turned, you're so out of control. Weaker vampires never evolve past this, not unlike humans in that sense, and rely solely on their base mind and instincts.

Compared to him, my slight toned features looked so fragile. He was well-built and tall with a dominating presence. His name suggested Nordic heritage, and I had no doubt just by looking at him that he was with his height, frame, and blue eyes. He had a closely cropped beard and long blonde hair that trailed down his back.

He must have been around my age when he was changed. He could be an imposing figure, but his charisma shone through so that he was warm and mischievous. Nothing malicious whatsoever. Peacefulness washed over me, and safety. Being there, under his protection, was soothing.

Sigurd laughed; he laughed a lot. And not due to cruel intentions or abject debauchery. He had honour, integrity. He taught me how to feed on the evil with compassion. His mind was sharp and his heart still held a glimmer of humanity within it. He had, I think, been a warrior a long, long time ago. His principles and humility had stood the test of time. A true warrior with a powerful disposition. Just what I needed—a conscientious vampire not caught up in the empty trappings of bloodlust and sex.

I asked Sigurd what he thought about my crimes. For some reason, I felt compelled and even safe pouring out all the wrongs I had done. I supposed as I respected him, I was hoping he'd grant me absolution or death. Either was preferable to my still vulnerable human/ vampire mind. I had hoped it would enrage him and he would kindly oblige to end my confusing life.

"Anthony, in my youth I killed many men whether it was for war or whatever reason. What is the difference? To kill, to take a life, to feel the power of wielding death upon another. What I learnt is this; it's how you live afterwards. You cannot undo what is done, and though, yes, you have hurt people, killed innocents, it is what you do next that matters most now. How you live your new life." His voice, robust and commanding, but not forceful, comforted my soul.

"And these innocent people, not so innocent, I think? Looking for sex, drugs, excitement? Let me tell you, Anthony, I have existed a long, long time. I tell you this; there are always people willing to tread into the dark corners of existence. To experience illicit pleasures, horrors, and deviance. You acted according to your base nature. It is quite normal for a new vampire; it is exciting and new. You could hardly have helped yourself. Your survival instinct is too strong. Those people were already lost, already dead inside when you found them. Their soul has long since been forgotten. The others you were with no doubt chose you for this. It is akin to a teenager finding their freedom for the first time. Now you can be so much more, and I don't mean here. You have to find your path. You have so much potential."

Then Sigurd laughed his deep warm laugh, and wrapped his arms around me and we slept, wrapped in each other's companionship as brothers in arms.

Sigurd had a lover, a human woman. It was some time before he allowed me to meet her. She was feisty just like him and laughed a great deal. She was beautiful and strong and playful, and I noticed that Sigurd never fed on her. To hear them together would wake the dead, and on those nights, I would wander the streets for many, many hours.

Her name was Tanya and she looked an English rose, though didn't act one. I liked her; she made me feel good about myself, always taking time for me.

And there I stayed for a while, learning to live again but without cruelty, debauchery. On occasion, he would disappear for a few nights and days, staying with his lover. I didn't know what she did for a living or where she lived, and I would never have presumed to ask. But we three were happy, and I absorbed the teachings, the warmth, and the love. It was like some dark medieval fairy tale. I poured out my anger in safety, after being plunged into this bloody existence which was not my choosing and the yearnings I held for my mortal life, my human lover, my friends.

His compassion and knowledge were soothing and in some ways, I felt relief in my tortured soul.

When the time came and I knew I had to leave, I also knew I would have to find them again in the future. But I was curious, I had to ask... "Sigurd, will you turn Tanya? You're so happy together. Or will you watch her grow old?"

"Tanya doesn't want it, Anthony, she likes the freedom and choice of being human. I wouldn't want to condemn her to this life, but if she asked and was sincere, I would happily do it. It would be selfish really, but I love her like no other and I would move Hell and high water just to be with her. So, I can only hope."

"Then I hope she does choose it, Sigurd, for you both."

"So, you're leaving to find your fate? Be careful, Anthony, there's a war out there." As he spoke, his lips tight and eyes small, warning me. He gestured, "Many vampires have gone missing and those that are found are neither vampire nor human, but wretched soulless beasts. I have seen things, not here but further off." And then he raised his voice, I had never heard him speak so seriously and with such authority. "Be sure to watch your back. You will always have a place here, a family, but out there, trust no one, understand? Tell no one of our meetings, or be sure I'll find you. Know I would die for my woman, so I value her safety above all else."

"Yes, I understand, Sigurd. I'll come back. And I'll be vigilant."

And so, ended like all things my tranquil time with my mentor and friend, and his lover. I could've stayed there forever, but I knew I had to find Tom and Josephine if they were still out there. And as Sigurd said, find my own destiny.

Dissolute Torture

Anthony

A CALMNESS AND SERENITY settled into me. Acceptance of myself; this creature. I would indeed feast on human blood, and forgive me, but this is my nature and not my will or choosing.

And so, I left to find my friends. But what I found took me to Heaven, then Hell.

I started searching, feeding on the less desirable beings and scanning bars and clubs. Though now I had the hindsight from Sigurd, it almost gave me permission to live out my natural desires, instincts. I took from the debauched, from those willing to surrender their soul and body to me, their blood. I stole from them what I needed with less shame than before. Then I came upon a clandestine group of vampires.

They asked me to join them for the night and although I had promised Sigurd I would be vigilant, their allure was too strong for me to pass up.

They were exquisite. They stood out amongst the mortals, and their leader, a curvaceous woman with emerald eyes and strawberry-blonde hair, enticed me into her.

"Come with us tonight. I want you and you in turn, can drink from me." Louisa whispered to me, her face against mine, lips brushing my face and her cool body pressed against me. It was cold, yet her clothing exposed much flesh, pale and luminous.

The others smiled as she ran her hand up my thigh. They didn't seem to care that we were in a club. My mouth went dry as her lips touched my face and as her hand traced my leg, my body trembled in excitement.

She led me outside to a darker place not far.

People were close by, yet she had no inhabitations. Running her hands down my body, she unzipped my trousers. "I want you," she murmured. So, I bathed in erotic shame, and all that I had learnt was lost then as I felt her, inhaled her. As I took her, she fed on my neck, sucking hard as the intensity of our lust grew. Swaying, I opened my eyes as she pulled away and put her wrist to my mouth.

I indulged myself in these strange women. Paradise was mine. Closing my eyes ecstasy took me over. And no guilt, no shame, just pure hedonism. I had no urge to open my eyes and I trembled with passion. I felt like I was falling into a trance of orgasmic sensation. I felt like I wasn't there anymore but somewhere else, with these vixens seducing my every desire.

Somewhere I had lost consciousness because I awoke with my hands chained above me and excruciating pain raging through me. Instinctively yelling out, my eyes adjusted to the dim lighting and I saw that I was in a large stone cellar. There was only a small barred window at one end, and the walls and floor were all bare stone. Shivering as the cold consumed me, I found I was stripped to the waist.

Two other vampires hung on the wall, arms above their head, chained. It was dark, their heads hung low so I couldn't see their faces but their scent was unforgettable.

I didn't know how long I had been like this, my feet were raised just off the ground so all my blood had drained to my feet.

Jolting in shock, convulsions shot through me as I became aware of where I was. Muscles tensed, rigid with fear. Sweat immediately broke out and my breathing became rapid.

What the hell had happened, how did I get here? It only seemed minutes ago that I was in sensual heaven. How the hell had I got here?

On the damp stonewalls of the cellar hung metal tipped whips, some barbed. Paddles with spikes, metal facemasks, and various cat of nine tails. On the floor in the corner, was a rack. Swallowing hard, my mouth completely dry, I lost my breath. *Did someone really use that?* Strewn across the place, bloodied hammers, evidence that indeed there was a sadistic bastard here, and as I looked the sweat continued to stream off me.

Amongst the devices lay skulls and bones of the less fortunate and the scent of blood was thick in the air.

I struggled crazily, screaming out, and tilting his head slightly towards me, Tom's eyes bruised and sullen. A shiver of fear passed through me. I had never seen him look like that, and as far as I knew, Tom was incredibly strong and hadn't known fear for a very long time.

"Where are we? What is this place? How did I get here?" I asked frantically. It took all my effort to speak, I felt so drained.

Tom and Josephine didn't answer. All hope stolen from their eyes, their souls lost, like men condemned to death.

This was it, I was about to pay for my heinous depraved acts.

But the thought persisted, how had I ended up here? Ah, Louisa. I couldn't help but smirk when I thought of her, what she had done to me. But that thought soon left me and now I was here in some dark-age nightmare.

Maybe it was hours that passed, I was not sure, but eventually a heavy door opened and three vampires entered. I remember thinking that the waiting was the worst part, the anticipation of torture, the fear. But I was wrong.

Alexander was to be more barbaric than I could have imagined and he eyed me with a yearning and distaste as one does when looking at an inferior being. I suffered a sense of dread that I had not known since before I was turned. Alexander was young when he was made vampire, about nineteen years old, his incandescent skin glowing. He was very slight with thick, dark curly hair. His ice-blue eyes provided a stark contrast to the black clothing he wore. He wore only designer black jeans and his pride, his gait tall and proud, self-assured.

Two female vampires, also noble in their demeanour and both older than him accompanied him. A small woman in her twenties I'd guess with short dark hair called herself Elizabeth. Dressed in modern clothes, she looked out of place in them. And Tabitha, a more voluptuous woman, taller and antiquely dressed in the absolute vampire colour, crimson. Tabitha's long dark hair looked striking against her snow-like complexion.

All three hovered around us, scrutinising us, their faces a mixture of fascination and disgust. They would hurt us for sure, but I also felt their growing sense of sexual intrigue, which left me chilled to the core. Would they beat us to a pulp and then bleed us dry?

And Alexander? The way he stared at me made me feel uneasy. He walked up to Tom and whispered something in his ear. Tom didn't even look up. Fear increased in me as Alexander's head tilted ever so slightly in my direction, and again he spoke quietly to Tom.

We do have acute hearing and no human can keep his or her whispered words from us, however quiet. Unfortunately, the same isn't true amongst our own kind.

After that, they all turned fast on their heels and left the cellar swiftly.

I had no idea how long we'd all been left, but I was weak from lack of blood, the pain of being chained up causing me to drift in and out of consciousness.

Alexander questioned me day after day. "Who made you?" he spat.

"I don't know, I was attacked!" I groaned. He picked up the club and beat me with it, against my side and stomach.

He continued in a rage of questions, his voice severe but steady. "How did you meet Tom and Josephine? Why did you take the lives of mortals?"

He battered me, punched me, and made me bleed for him. Grabbing my wrist, bit, and drank my blood whilst staring me in the eyes, a slight grin on his immaculate face. He was delighted by my pain and aroused by it. A psychotic vampire. What the fuck would I do now? He amused himself greatly with his psychological games and torture. His behaviour became more frenzied and he would press himself upon me, wicked and extreme as he was.

Josephine and Tom suffered much the same and it was obvious that Alexander and his "group" had been trying to catch them for a long time.

"You realise you put us all in jeopardy?" he shouted at us. "You shall all pay." Laughing he said, "But we shall not kill you. No. We have other plans for you. You will be of use to us." Like Nathaniel before him, Alexander spoke with exacting English, eloquent and determined.

Days passed and we heard or saw nothing from any of them. We could barely talk, so weak. Our fate seemed doomed and God only knew what they had planned for us, if not death. Blood for others perhaps? Being drained to death. We were left in that cellar amongst the smell of blood; chained, beaten, and wondering what he would do to us next.

I awoke to agony on my inner thigh and a piercing sting on my neck, that familiar pain. With a start, I opened my eyes to find Tabitha feeding on my thigh and Alexander feeding on my neck. My clothes were gone and they were aroused. I thought in that instant that I could drain them and escape. But I was too sore from the torture. Aching and broken.

The weakness washed over me. I hadn't fed for so long. I glanced wearily over at Tom and Josephine. I'd have to help them, I couldn't be without them, not after all we'd been through. They were my evil kindred spirits, but then I thought of Sigurd. They were not my friends, their encouragement was what I was now being punished for, and I could leave them here in their wickedness and terror together.

Then I forgot everything. They loosened my chains and Alexander kicked me, forcing me to the ground. I looked into his eyes. This wasn't what I wanted, but Alexander had other ideas.

He dragged me by the back of my neck across the bloody stone floor and tossed me down. Their advances were assaulting, vicious, and strong. They took turns in their depraved fantasies. I was like a rag doll bandied around, used, and thrown about.

They kicked me, beat me, bled me, and fed on me. Their shrill laughter chilled me to the bone. I knew my time had come, but it was such agony. Was this how my victims had felt? I was so powerless, battered, and bruised, filthy, and wallowing. It was surreal.

Unconsciousness was again my only salvation releasing me from suffering, and the thirst being so harsh that I only have vague memories of sensations of that time. That twisted, dark nightmare. I was in Hell on earth.

He dragged me along with a chain around my neck, Alexander looking hideously angry. The suffering was constant and agonising. Then Alexander was suddenly calm, all his violent anger gone and my body went cold and rigid with terror. Gulping for air, my legs shook and I trembled uncontrollably. Blurred vision, I reached out for something, anything to stabilize me. I found nothing. There was to be no redemption for me.

Tabitha approached me, her mouth curved like a scythe, small eyes watching me, evil intent. She stripped naked, then placed herself onto me. Cold eyes looked right through me, but that smirk remained, I had to look away. She looked awful in her power and writhed around, laughing, grinding into me. Letting out an almighty yell that pained my ears, shrill and rasping, she laughed and I was so raw. So sore. Alexander stood there, watching me, no expression on his striking face.

He grabbed the back of her head, pulled her off of me. Looking at me, he then spun her around and kissed her fiercely.

I wondered why he had given me his blood unless it was to keep me alive a bit longer for his torment. It made my stomach spasm and I ended up coughing back out more than I could ingest. I wanted death; this was all that could release me now.

I had no compulsion to escape their advances, they were too strong, and I was too sick. I hoped, at least, that the worst was over now. I would have prayed, but I don't think God would hear me. I knew I was beyond saving. I hated this life, this mess, these fiends. If I had an eternity to become this, I would choose fire instead. Nothing can escape fire.

Alexander grabbed me by the arms, led me back to the wall, put me in chains, and left with Tabitha.

I have no idea how long this lasted, days I think, but the pain, the stench, the thought of them repeating this at any time drove my mind crazy. Hardly able to breath, shock took me over in its entirety. I was broken.

Alexander was confidently complacent regarding his safety and my powerlessness. After drinking his blood, slowly I became stronger but also nauseous. It was not normal. I could drink other vampire blood, and even though his blood had made me ill, I at least gained some power from it. Causing me to convulse from time to time, and it took what energy I had left to contain my discomfort when he entered the room.

The routine was the same; he came in alone and walked up to me. He would whisper something in my ear and brush my face with his lips. I knew he was toying with me. I could not keep physically or mentally enduring this. His games made me snap. Literally.

Maybe a vampire cornered and in fear of his life will fight to the death and find some untapped inner strength.

As his lips brushed my face and he whispered softly in my ear, I locked my mouth onto his neck and sucked so hard, so fast that his legs weakened. I bit as hard as I could.

He pulled away and I held fast. I tore his flesh as my bite remained fixed at his neck and he went down. His strong blood coursed through my veins. I could feel my strength returning, and my muscles pumping that elixir fast through me. This was my only chance. I made an almighty pull on the chains and they loosened slightly, and I grabbed at Alexander who was screaming in agony as half his flesh was left in my mouth.

I grabbed him, wrists rattling in their shackles, and drank and drank. Immediately, my stomach tightened and I felt sick, but I fought through this. I pulled him and myself away from the wall. Nausea hit me as I clung to him; the bolts began to loosen away from the stone. I felt frantic, crazed. My grip around his neck held firm. Suddenly, we lunged forward as the bolts shot free and I stumbled onto him as we lost our footing. I grabbed at a metal rod that he had left carelessly on the floor and before I'd realised what I'd done, I'd impaled it through his dying body. It all happened in a second. Tom and Josephine were wide-eyed, their faces full of shock.

I grabbed at the keys on his belt, my bloodied hands slipping, unable to grip them. Panting, shaking I finally grasped them and clumsily unlocked the chains from my wrists. Stumbling towards to Tom and Josephine, I clenched the keys tight trying to keep my grip to unlock them. Convulsions spasmed through me, from his foul blood that tore at my insides and it was all I could do to stop myself from hurling.

Alexander writhed around, blood pouring from his stomach like a violent waterfall, overflowing. His groans grew fainter as the blood gushed onto the floor. I knew those vicious women would be in at any second. But the more I hurried, the more I fumbled. My hands were sticky and slippery with his blood. I could feel my heart pounding and my breathing was heavy. I had to get out, I had to get out.

We hurried out, running as fast as we could until Tom found a car. He was desperate in his attempt and took ages to hot-wire it. It started, cut out. Panic grew inside me, dread fast and swift that we might be caught. Sweat poured from me as I watched in horror as Tom constantly failed at hot-wiring a car. Eventually, it started and then he slammed his foot down and we didn't stop until dawn. Then we collapsed.

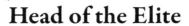

Head of the Elite

Tyrell

FOR THREE CENTURIES, I have been Head of the Elite Coven of Vampires and in that time, I have watched in revulsion as our kind has become a useless, corrupt, inept species, and I shall tolerate it no more.

Until now, I didn't have the means to stop this over-spill of worthless creatures, breeding and out of control. There are too many. I shall return our species to the old order where only select vampires are granted permission to change mortals to vampires, as for the rest...They will either comply or die. Now I have genetics to aid this and the start of a new order.

When I got news that my son had been attacked and left for dead, and the vicious bastards that did this got away! I had sent Alexander to detain some malcontents, Tom and Josephine and their new sidekick, a young deviant, Anthony. My steward informed me tentatively. Rage bellowed through me like wild-fire and the incompetence of everyone around me, their utter uselessness.

"What do you mean they got away? Get Alexander, I don't care what's happened, bring him here, *now*. He is my son and I will restore him if it takes the blood of a thousand vampires to do it. *Go*," I roared. My anger erupted out, furiously.

"And get Emidius! I want her here," I thundered as I watched Nicolas, my steward, rushing off to fulfil my orders.

Obstinately, Nicolas spun around and called out, his voice shaking, "Professor, we can't just *summon* her; it's not in her nature to be summoned. Remember last time?" Nicolas's voice was strangled in fear and anticipation of summoning Emidius, and this protest enraged me even more.

"Nicolas, bring me Emidius. I do not employ you to think." It was as if the world had gone mad, me, being questioned by my own servant! "Once you've completed these tasks, I want a full report progress on my project, is that clear?"

Yes, now he trembled and so he should, with his head bowed.

"How many have we lost this week?"

"None, Professor, we are at last making progress, but it's not consistent."

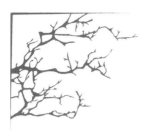

Chains

Jamie

LOCKED IN A CELL AND I didn't know why I was here. What crime had I committed? My maker never told me about this. I hadn't done anything wrong.

I got up, screamed at the tiny gap through the door of the padded cell. I didn't detect much human scent, so I reasoned I couldn't be in a regular prison. Screaming for answers, for a reason why I was here, but it was all met with silence. My throat was sore and dry from shouting. High above me, a slight breeze whispered in revealing a barred window. I had been able to use the metal bed frame, placed upside down against the padded walls and scampered up to move the bars slightly, but not enough for even a cat to get though. Now my stomach spasmed, I was starving and my strength was disappearing fast. I drifted in and out of awareness.

I'd been turned five years ago. Until finding myself here, I was happy all the time, hence my laughter lines.

My past, I used to work in writing computer programmes and I enjoyed it. My weekends were all playing sports, rugby mainly and out with my friends chasing women. Just before I was changed, I'd met a woman who wowed me, and I thought, this is it! After years of dating, I'd finally met her.

My life was similar to yours; I worked, looked forward to Fridays and enjoyed lazy Sundays.

It was a Saturday night, I was meant to meet with Alice, the woman who made me quiver. Walking to the restaurant in the city, I met my maker.

Cunning as she was, she appeared to need help with her car, bonnet up and whilst starting the engine it hissed and whirred. Obviously, I offered to help.

As she spoke to me distressed and panicked, I was unable to look away from her. Transfixed, staring into her eyes, something compelled me to her, like an invisible cord was pulling me into her. Even now, in this place of hell, I remember her exact words as she moved close to me. Feeling her breath on my neck, her lips brushed my skin sending shivers through my body.

"Jamie, delicious Jamie. I have been watching you for many months. You are beautiful, charming and mine. Come to me." Opening her arms, I walked blindly into them, into her sensuality, desire driving through me.

Smiling now, I was glad that we made love that night, before I was changed. To have that experience with her as a human, then a vampire. I was utterly and completely addicted to her. To being with her, and tasting her rich blood. Older blood smells stronger and tastes bitter. Just thinking of her now...but that was five years ago. When she left me, she just disappeared and I was at a loss.

I stayed in her house, as a vampire I'd lost all my human friends, my family, my belongings. It took me a long time to get over her. I'm not sure I ever really did.

I can't contemplate my future right now. Just the present and how the fuck to get out. *Why* am I here? I'd heard the rumours, like everyone else, of some Elite group rounding up and killing vampires, but I also knew that most of the vampires that went missing had a reputation for viciousness. I did not. Bath is a small city and it's impossible not to know your vampire neighbours.

Either way, it didn't bode well. After the few days of my trying to reason, trying to get an answer or any response, my mind started to play tricks on me and my reason faltered. The screams I heard were terrifying, sounds of torture followed by the silence. That silence leaving me shivering with fear. And emptiness being isolated. Hunched in the corner on the floor I couldn't stop shaking. Fear embraced me and my body ached in discomfort from it and from starvation. Crouching in the filth of the cell, with only that small, barred window high up on the wall allowed a meagre amount of light and air in. Soiled clothes, thirst, and uncertainty filled me with revulsion and panic. I was determined though that I would find a way out or die trying. I cried until I had no blood left to spill.

As I sat in the filth and isolation of that place, getting out seemed more remote and starving to death appeared to be my punishment. As this realisation took hold, my hope plunged into blackness, an abyss of emptiness, dying alone and no one would know it. Not even my maker, if she cared.

Something startled me, I imagined that the door was opening- it took me a few minutes to realise that I wasn't dreaming as two guards, dressed all in black pulled me up by my shoulders. Too weak to stand from starvation, they dragged me out but it was hazy. Slipping in and out of a dream state, I saw a chubby older man with a high receding hairline. I remember thinking, I sense he's vampire but it's odd, vampires are usually chosen for their looks above all else, above character. It made me smile, he watched me intently. An incredulous stare, his gaze fixed on me. But I sensed no malice.

Too weak even to ask where I was being taken, they carried me off up stone steps, through cold, grey corridors that in my state all looked the same until eventually I felt my body being lifted and relaxing on a bed of sorts. Then I just shut my eyes; let what will happen, happen. I don't care anymore.

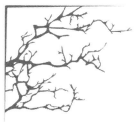

Mutation

Tyrell

AFTER MY SON WAS BRUTALLY injured, my passion for the elimination of the underclass became magnified. They deserve nothing less than annihilation.

I knew that wiping out en masse of an entire species was impossible so using my skill and my connections, I had studied gene therapy and I was taught by the best.

Science had always fascinated me, and I have seen it develop into a type of religion in human kind. Curious that anything they don't understand in science, they dismiss. Idiots!

The process we were instilling was gene therapy. As we, the Elite class have a purer strain of the bacterium, the infection that long ago made us vampires. This bacterium is ancient, some say as old as the Earth itself. I injected my subjects with a sample of the bacterium taken from some chosen few of the Elite and spliced it into their genes. Like Natural Selection, not all adapt, the weak die, or become the experimentals which I keep for study or donor use. Those that die, we burn.

A purer class of immortals, stronger, more intelligent, faster. When the hosts' bodies accepted it, their muscle density increases along with their vision and hearing improves tenfold, resulting in their physiology becoming more powerful beyond human recognition.

Lesser vampires are ill-bred and cannot sustain the purity and strength of the higher class, that is no concern of mine.

In my day, the majority of vampires were carefully selected. And all but a very few stuck to the rules. I am, of course, of aristocratic blood, but even other higher vampires from less established human bloodlines could hold an untainted vampire lineage, if carefully chosen.

Once the bacterium is injected into the host, it takes just thirty hours for it to infiltrate every gene, every cell, and either alter these beyond recognition, or the cells start to split and the body rejects it, starting a slow and painful death. However, as they were already a vampire and held a weaker version of the infection, their breakdown, both physical and mental, is extreme and prolonged.

The Making of Gods

Jamie

SLOWLY OPENING MY EYES, flickers of light danced before me. Swooping, bursting with trails, I thought I was hallucinating. Strength and virility pumped through my body, stronger than before, nothing felt the same or smelt the same. Even in my drowsy state, I was aware of men and vampires standing around me. Strapped down and yet I just knew the power I possessed, I could break the bonds, but for now, now I would just lie here. Drugged. Swimming in my mind.

"All his signs are good. Nicolas, get him some blood," the voice was sharp, authoritative. "This one, this one is exceptional," the same voice said.

Are they talking about me?

Gasping, my body rose up slightly, involuntarily as a large needle plunged into my arm and I felt with precision as a hot liquid coursed through my veins.

"We'll want to keep this one pure, Nicolas," the voice said again. "He requires a good source of food, nothing dismal. See to it." Then he bent over my face and I felt his warm breath over me as he whispered, "Perfection..."

Again, the voice stated over me, loudly this time, "You! Take him to the east quarters. See that he's comfortable."

Later, I lay there in my plush quarters staring at the ceiling, incredulous sensations flowing through my body like electricity. At last, I sat up, with the power of a God.

What the...?

A force pumped through me, my body energised, charged to a new level. I felt like I could leap off a building. Invincible. The sensation of eyes boring into me. Somewhere in this room, someone was monitoring me.

What have they done to me, and more worryingly, why? My attention drawn to the barred window. A big window in a beautiful room richly decorated, with 19th century furnishing, but it fitted the room. Heavy drapes fell on either side of the window and thick rugs, richly designed, carpeted the wooden floor.

Getting off the bed, I gazed outside; the whole world looked different, more animated, more alive.

I was aware of the ever-present life force pulsating in all living things. Of the sounds of nature.

My hands, my skin. I gazed at myself. My blood pumped faster and looked luminescent through my tanned skin. I felt like Narcissus, spellbound by the magnificence of my new reflection. I couldn't stop staring at myself.

As I moved towards the mirror, I was transfixed by my eyes. *God, what the...* My eyes were almost completely black. But my vision... With that, I turned and before I knew it I was gazing outside, seeing everything, the likes of which I'd never seen before.

I could *sense* a man called Nicolas. His name popped into my mind, and I knew he was coming to see me. Then I heard his footsteps, I felt his intention. I stood fascinated, staring at the door handle.

Nicolas turned the handle to my room with trepidation. Although an old vampire and strong, all his instincts told him that he would be no match for me. I sensed his emotions, he feared and envied me. Wobbling a little as my mind tried to make sense that I could actually feel what another was feeling.

Bound, gagged, and sedated beside Nicolas was a woman. She was young with short red hair and red-stained lips. A pale and shapely vampire, she looked quite noble in her dress.

"Jamie." Nicolas tried to sound commanding. "We thought you might be hungry."

"Oh, it was you in that room? I see. Thank you, I think." I felt uneasy, like I was high on drugs. Nothing seemed real. Even the texture of the soft rug beneath my bare feet felt surreal, like walking on cotton wool, soft and bouncy. And I found that once I realised something, once I was aware of a sensation, I fixated upon it.

"Human blood may not suffice your tastes now. You might want something more potent." Nicolas handed the girl over to me and I took her with fascination. I could smell her blood so clearly, see it coursing through her veins and hear the thrumming of her heart beating. Gazing at her like a cat that looks upon its prey with excitement and infatuation.

In seconds as I started to drink her, my libido raged inside me. I pushed her to my bed, our eyes locked, vampire to vampire, revelling in such a heightened sensation of lust. Every touch, every kiss seemed magnified in its feeling on my skin, tingling, like warm fizzy water filling every area of my body. Breath-taking. But wrapped in euphoria I was slow to realise that the girl was dead. I'd drained her completely and she fell out of my arms, rolled lifelessly off the bed, thudding to the floor.

I jolted back shocked, horrifically and peculiarly I wasn't *that* upset. I knew I should be. Remorse ought to be consuming me. I'd never killed. That's who I was. And yet, and yet. An empty sensation of compassion fell over me, but was replaced but a stronger emotion of superiority; like this was my birth right, the natural order.

"Nicolas!" I bellowed.

And I knew, I sensed that Nicolas had been watching from the hidden camera. He arrived quickly, puffing slightly with his security staff and I detected a heightened emotion of fear; he expected me to create trouble regarding the loss of my humanity. I realised in that moment that I could smell the fear from him, and hear his racing heart as he approached my room. Before, as a vampire, without whatever they'd done to me, I could smell fear and malevolence in humans. But here, now this was stronger so that before he even entered the room my senses were keen, I gasped at the acknowledgement of that.

"Nicolas," I spoke softly, not in the least self-conscious about my being naked. "I need more. I am sorry, I drained her. I need another... Please."

Although I wasn't sorry, and my desire outweighed my compassion right now.

"That's alright, Jamie. Daniel, get another. Maybe an older vampire." And turning to me he spoke in an almost fatherly way, "Those who have been vampire longer often have stronger blood, I shall keep this in mind." Then turning to the guards,

"Quickly now, bring one." Then Nicolas gestured with his hand over the corpse and the guards carried away the dead vampire.

The new woman was brought immediately and not sedated. She thrashed and cursed, restrained in titanium handcuffs. She stopped once she saw me. My blonde hair, lean tanned body, waiting for her with blood running down my face and chest. I held out my hand to her, our eyes locked, and Nicolas shut the door.

Summon the Goddess

Emidius

"TYRELL, YOUR INSOLENCE has pushed me too far. How dare you summon me! I shall tear you into a thousand pieces if you ever summon me again! I hope for your sake that your reason is great," I shrieked. The sound was deafening and to a mortal, their eardrums would shatter, and that effect wasn't dissimilar for a vampire. But I liked to keep Tyrell in his place, as he so delighted in doing this to all others.

He feigned composure. Falling on his knees to mark his respect, knowing I could wipe them out in one easy swoop of my power; and though he despised kneeling to anyone or anything, he was desperate.

"Great Emidius, forgive me, I beg your help. My son, my only son has been killed. I beg of you, please help me bring him back. I will pay *any* price." His words, slow, loud, and deliberate. He was crying, his salty bloody tears mixed as he knelt on the stone floor at my feet, a proud man now distressed and humbled, made to beg for the life of his only beloved son. I almost felt compassion for him. He was obviously genuine, I had never known him to beg anyone, ever.

He was a mad despot. He had been for many an age, but I had seen worse than him in my thousands of years. *Though he is insignificant, it's better to have him in charge than something far worse.*

My power is great, greater than any other being. There are a few others like me and together we are formidable. Not human and yet not god, but a demi-god. No other being knew what they were. Those few who knowingly encountered us knew we took human form, but they also knew we could take any shape.

It is said, that when you feel a cold shiver for no reason, that it is the whisper of an immortal passing near.

Judgement on mortals and immortals alike fell to me and my kind. I tolerated the vampires, the lesser immortals. They were so ancient, understanding the natural order of predator and prey. By tolerating them, I gained some control over them. It was me and my kind that forbade the killing of innocents, long, long ago.

We had summoned the lower beings, vampires amongst others, and convened a truce that we, the half-gods, would not destroy the vampires if the vampires hunted only evil humans. A pact that the vampires readily agreed to, for like humans whose desire for evil is insatiable, the vampires desire for human blood is also insatiable.

But now, in the twenty-first century, the rise in numbers of vampires spiralled out of control. Many were malicious, bold, and took any human they so desired. It would not be long before their existence would become known, and that would spell disaster.

So, I listened to Tyrell.

Tyrell was old and although I neither liked nor trusted him, I needed him and his council to keep control.

"I will help you, Tyrell, but there will be a price. When I have decided that price, you will pay. You will bring your son here on the full moon and I will need the blood of thirteen vampires. And Tyrell, choose well. I will also require some of your blood and the blood of *the vicious strain*. You know of what I speak... And Tyrell," and here I paused to make my point, "they must all be alive when I arrive."

I knew that appeasing Tyrell and keeping him in my debt was to my advantage. "Now," I commanded. "I want to see your project. Take me there." Though I knew what he was doing here, I wanted to see it for myself.

He led me down the narrow stone steps into the bleak stinking cellars beneath the complex. The place was sparse and threatening.

I made no comment on the horror I witnessed, I just listened to his explanations, his excuses for the 'experimentals' he called them, that after his failings of gene splicing they were neither human nor vampire. Throwing themselves at their cell doors, wailing like banshees, eyes wide with fear and confusion. I showed no emotion, these creatures would tear you to shreds and not comprehend a thing, of that I was sure of. Simply, I shook my head, they were once human, but humans after all are the most dangerous of creatures. Tyrell had been human, then vampire and I judged what he had done to his own kin. That was obviously the human side of vampire nature, there was no reason to point it out to him, he would argue for his own limitations. He led me back up to the complex, upstairs to his best accomplishment.

"Emidius, this is our greatest success." As Tyrell opened the door, he introduced me. "Emidius meet Jamie, the leader of our Elite Army. Jamie, meet Emidius. Kneel, Jamie, kneel to her devastating power."

Jamie did not respond as Tyrell expected. He did not lower his eyes to his superiors. In fact, he looked straight at me and I watched as he swayed a little, what they had done to him allowed him to feel my energy. He was unlike any other vampire. A hybrid genetically altered with the strongest source of the infection from Tyrell's pure and ancient lineage. Unlike Tyrell, he was young and fit and had the sharp mind of those of this age.

The vampire he had fed on lay dead on the floor and Tyrell pointed silently to his guards to remove the corpse. Jamie awkwardly knelt before me and was still naked as if it did not occur to him to be clothed.

"Tyrell, leave us." I whispered.

Tyrell's army was growing. Those that failed the therapy were either studied or incinerated at the facilities crematorium. Soon he would have a hundred unsurpassed vampires that would guard them and wipe out all the lesser, vagrant vampires that were polluting the land.

In Tyrell's mind, this was not genocide. It was order. It was survival. It was the beginning.

But for now, my mind rested on studying Jamie. To see just how powerful, he really was.

Blood of the Gods

Emidius

TYRELL HAD A ROOM PREPARED for the ceremony to restore his son. Alexander was somewhere between life and death after his attack. Tyrell's face betrayed his emotion as Alexander's lifeless body was brought in and placed on an altar at the end of the room.

In all the time I had known Tyrell I had never seen him display emotion openly and had thought him incapable of feeling.

The room was large and square with stone pillars within. The huge windows had heavy drapes pulled together, and black candles filled the room, as I'd requested, the only lighting to be allowed. Incense burned, the air was smoky and thick with the sweet scent.

A blazing fire filled the large stone fireplace and the flames caressed the surroundings, inviting and warm. The complex was old and the fire was the only heating, so this fire had been built with care to sustain the ritual. Pictures on the wall, as old as the complex, were masked in shadow with the candlelight flickering on them, but aside from its contents of immortals, the room itself gave a serene feeling.

Thirteen vampires stood chained together in groups around pillars to prevent them from moving within the room. At the largest central pillar, with enough sedation to floor an elephant, and standing amongst an overkill of titanium chains stood the beast, the one they would not name. For even Tyrell feared such a beast. A true immortal, it slouched, massive, its muscular mass oppressive to look at. Its breathing was heavy and heaving and in its sedated state, saliva drooled from its powerful jaws.

The thirteen were noisy and aggressive, restrained and chained in cuffs, their feet in shackles. Their anxiety was tangible, ashen faces, shrill voices, beads of sweat pouring off their dead faces. Most were shaking, pleading and as I eyed them, their voices trembled all the more, begging for release.

Panic spread as they eyed the beast and Alexander. They saw their fate before them, argued with the guards, shouting, asking why they were here. What crime had they committed? That this was a medieval travesty. They shouted and demanded justice, for the Elite to abide by their own rules, but it was all in vain. The guards were ordered to make no contact with them, not even eye contact.

Once I saw that everything was in place, I summoned all to leave with a sweeping gesture of my hand. Tyrell, who had been in there all along overseeing the arrangements, did not stop to argue. Not when his son's life hung in the balance.

I walked over to the thirteen and as they shouted obscenities at me or pleaded, I simply moved my flat, outstretched hand in front of their faces and they fell silent. As if sleeping, but their eyes wide open in a trance-like state.

Slowly, I walked to the beast. Treading lightly, I was aware, it had started to awaken.

"Who are you?" I whispered.

Its eyes opened slightly and it let out a shrill howl that screamed like nails on a chalkboard throughout the complex.

"No matter now, you shall find peace tonight, my friend," I muttered, again waving my hand in front of its face, pale blue light radiating out from it, and falling like dew upon its face. The beast fell silent.

"Ichor, the blood of thirteen immortals is needed to charge the life force of the one called Alexander," I called before the altar. My arms outstretched beckoning to the Gods. "Great star Sirius, look with favour as I spill the blood of thirteen immortals and of this beast. Look with favour and give this boy another chance at immortality. So mote it be."

I took the silver chalice and the dagger to each of the vampires who were still in a daze, and slit their wrists until a few drops of blood from each of them fell into the chalice. Then to the beast. Sadness overcame me as I cut its wrist and the thick dark blood fell into the cup. *This creature is so tortured.* Taking the blood-filled chalice to Alexander, and tipping it carefully, I slowly trickled the blood into his mouth, one drop at a time. I waited. Calmness surrounded me here, tranquillity.

Alexander slowly showed signs of movement. His eyes darted under the heavy lids, his body twitched lightly. I continued to drip-feed him the blood of the immortals. The thirteen hung limply around the pillars, their chains bound together, preventing them from completely slumping against the floor.

The beast, however, looked a sorry state. Once a magnificent creature capable of putting the fear of God into even the

Elite, now it was a collapsed carcass, blood pooled around its base.

The smell of blood and incense and the heat from the fire smothered the air, wrapped in magic, a familiar smell of old witchcraft.

Still, I continued to drip the blood into the boy's mouth, one drop at a time and observing the ever-so-slight movements. Flickering eyes, the corners of his lips. He was an evil bastard for sure, but he was beautiful. Not in a masculine way, in a boy-ish way, streamlined, sleek, innocent looking. He had used his beauty to gain whatever he wanted from whomever he wanted. Stopping for a while, I traced my fingers over the high cheek-bones. He was starting to revive now. The large hole was mending, the skin fusing, white blood cells rushing in urgency to close and heal the wound.

Ichor. Only thought of as a legend. I was glad, however, that I had not used the blood of actual gods. I would not even contemplate that, especially with one so cruel. But thirteen immortals and the beast, that would be enough to restore him to his former glory. Gazing at him, Alexander looked so innocent, so young. He had been born of a human mother and Tyrell had somehow fathered him, or so the story went, and I doubted that. Tyrell's son. I was distracted then by his sudden intake of breath, a gasp. At last, he had consumed all the blood. Leaning over him closely, I inhaled his scent.

Why are you so evil? What happened to you? Then I turned to face the altar on which he lay and placing the chalice down, opened my arms once more to beckons the Gods.

"Great Sirius now so near to this Earth. I call upon the powers of divine life to restore this boy. Give him life once more." Here I paused. "But, temper him with humility. And I make this pact now; if he acts evil, then take his life. Take it quickly and take the life of his father. So mote it be."

Lowering my arms, I sighed, distracted by the vampire before me. In all my years, I had seen many a charming vampire, and sometimes human. He was exceptional. Little wonder why Tyrell wanted him saved. Now I hung back for in my heart I already knew his fate. Just as I knew Jamie's and I liked Jamie. My mind drifted as I pondered that concept. I am neither human nor supernatural, yet I felt some semblance of emotion.

Why was that? For a long time, I hadn't felt anything. I had existed in a neutral state until I saw Jamie. As I stood there thinking, the time passed slowly like clouds drifting. Then Alexander opened his eyes.

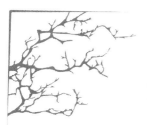

Running

Anthony

"TOM, JOSEPHINE, WAKE up, we've got to move!" I blurted. We had slept for hours in this dark, damp place. I noticed a foul smell and realised that the stench was us. I shook Tom and Josephine, but they were out cold. I knew that they might sleep longer yet, so I stumbled out of our hiding place to look for blood.

As I staggered out of the stinking crypt, I looked around. I couldn't remember where I was, then the flashback of what had happened to me and what I had done hit me. At the same time, a violent stabbing pain in my stomach caused me to double over.

Was this hunger? Falling on my knees I held my stomach, trying hard not to scream out in pain. I crawled on the damp grass, but the pain was too much and I lay there amongst the meadow staring up at the night's sky, holding my knees up to my chest to try to curb the hurt. I hadn't looked at the sky in a long time and as my mind drifted, the pain seemed to lessen. I laughed at my life, whatever it was. But I felt an ease just gazing at the night sky.

I could stay here forever, I mused to myself. That thought felt so peaceful, so calm. Just stay here, needing nothing. Wanting no one. Just being.

I had killed some noble vampire freak after debauching most of the population of Bath. I had killed. I had lost the love of my life and now I was here outside a crypt, hiding from God-knows-what, covered in crap and stinking like some foul creature from the bowels of Hell.

I laughed in a frenzy as my mind went spinning.

"How appropriate," I called to no one. "I am a child of the devil. I am living Hell. I deserve this agony." With that, I lurched over in pain crying out, scrunching up my knees tighter to my chest. *I can't run anymore. I am staying here when the sun rises. Who cares... Let whoever find me. I deserve my fate. They deserve their vengeance. I just want to die here.*

And I wished at that moment that the legends were true so that I could just lay here until dawn and burn in the sun. And keep this beloved peace.

Tom found me first. "Anthony, Anthony, come on, we've got to get out of here. Josephine, help me," Tom called.

I lay there grinning, but unable to move. "Leave me," I growled.

Tom and Josephine looked the worse for wear, and I had no doubt they, too, were in discomfort. Dawn was nearing and my torment was intense. "This is retribution for the suffering I've caused. Leave me here to die. I don't want to go on," I groaned.

"We'd better take him back in the crypt," Tom said, and he and Josephine carried me in.

They ignored my cries completely. "I could try," Josephine said, "I know I've not fed, but I'm better than Anthony."

Tom hesitated and nodded.

She bit her wrist and placed it over my mouth.

Rather than a steady flow of thick blood, it trickled uneasily and tasted weak, thinned. I would not drink, could not. Take her life as well? Maybe she had used me, but I wouldn't find my redemption by taking her life. I refused steadfastly until she grabbed the back of my head and forced her wrist to my mouth. Her face was stern, eyes narrowed and furrowed forehead in offence of my refusal.

Tom shot off to some nearby houses, certain to find something evil to bring back and eat. Unfortunately, there was almost always a rotten human where there were people. Be it addiction, violence, emotional abuse. One thing was for sure; he'd find the worst one and bring it back.

I drank from Josephine reluctantly. As her blood slowly oozed into my mouth, my anguish eased a little. I felt warmer now and safer. My head swam in that cold, dark, damp crypt, Josephine's blood intoxicating me all the while.

Why had Alexander's blood made me so ill? As I sat there drinking I lost track of time.

Tom returned with a worn-looking man, at a guess in his late thirties, though in truth he appeared twenty years older. Haggard by alcohol, his face was deep with lines and saggy with excess skin. Puffy eyes with dark circles, the man tumbled in, falling over his own weight. A sorry state of a human being. You can smell the bad ones; it's as if they carry their own unique evil scent. He had lost any spark of life to the bottle. We could all *feel* that this man was aggressive. We could smell the malevolence emanating from him like some foul aroma.

It made us feel better to feed on useless, aggressive people. It awakens our primal instincts.

Another time we would have sent him off, telling him to run. Then we would have hunted him down, toyed with him, put the fear of God into him, and fed from him. All the while, he would be unable to move, but he would be fully conscious that he was our victim this time. He would feel his life slipping away, and with every gulp, we would end the terror of his victims' lives. Or so we thought in our righteous minds. But then we like to show them that there are bigger, more powerful predators out there, watching, waiting for the ones like him.

But now, they just drank him and fed off his fear. It enlivened them. But for me, I felt sorrow for the man. What causes a boy so full of vibrant life to become that angry, so lost, so wasted?

"Blood full of hate," Tom muttered. He pushed the haggard man towards Josephine and the man fell before her on his knees. She lifted his wrist whilst staring looking straight into his tired eyes and bit. Tom grabbed at the other.

They fed like greedy children and I watched as the life drained slowly out of him. Another victim bled dry.

Josephine shot me a fierce look and meandered over to me. "Here, have some more," she said, offering me her neck. I took her, both of us stinking, bloody and dirty. It made me feel carnal, primal. But this time I felt different. Virile and pumped but with no affection, just animalistic instinct.

She wanted sex, that was all. No emotion. The blood lust fuelled my hunger, and I followed it without regard. I knew then that whatever lay in store for me, this was not what I wanted. It was an empty existence. I would release this torrent within me without feeling. Tom grabbed the back of my head by my hair and in passion pushed me aside.

Three of us in our depraved obsession totally unaware that we were being watched. When we realised it was too late.

Wrapped up in our shame, the noise of a safety release on a gun made us jolt around to see a militia force surrounded us with weapons. Lots of weapons.

Stopping suddenly, awestruck at the soldiers. They were vampires and I remember the urban myths told to me by Sigurd.

They were striking, black military combats, weapons, boots, organised. We, on the other hand were stupefied, naked, shamed, and very vulnerable.

A striking blonde vampire strode over to us with such confidence and charisma, he made me feel even more foolish. He stood there for a minute or two before he spoke, eyeing each of us, mainly Josephine. He showed absolutely no emotion in his face, just stood there glaring. I could see he was aroused, and I could see she wanted him. But he was able to contain himself with such eloquence.

"You," he said to Josephine. "Get up slowly." His voice was soft yet deep with authority. He looked like a golden statue.

Josephine obeyed straight away, out of character and moved transfixed to him. He walked up to her, his eyes tracing her naked body and he stood a hair's breadth away.

"We have come to take you, all of you," he said calmly. "You are all in deep shit. Though judging by this human, I ought to kill you all where you stand. *Why* is the human dead?" With the last word, it seemed he was drawn away from his lust and into the horror of the situation. I was intrigued by that, by his morality.

"He's a violent abuser to others. He's of no concern to anyone. We did society a favour," Tom snapped sharply.

"And yet." He paused for effect, and then slowly drawing out each word continued, "It *is* forbidden, Tom. Why didn't you just weaken him and distort his mind, as you usually do, to stop him hurting others? It really is stupid to kill your dinner. You, of all people, know the penalty, I think?"

"How do you know what I usually do, and who the fuck are you anyhow?" Tom lashed out. Tom's mouth had tightened and his eyes looked hard into this creature of power. But the soldier was completely unfazed.

"Ah, Tom. I know all about you," this golden-haired vampire said, striding towards him. There was no hatred in his eyes, just curiosity.

"Who... are... you, what do you want with... us?" I stammered, though, in truth, I had an idea what he was, I was scared to find out.

"Anthony," he said and looked right into my soul. "Yes, Anthony. You have quite a reputation for one so young. You are screwed, my friend. You see, Alexander is an Elite vampire with *the* most powerful father. I am sorry to have to say it, but I do not like the thought of your fate. Shame, for one so young. Still..."

"Alexander's a psycho!" I yelled. "The freak chained us up, abused us, tortured us!"

"And you did what to the mortals, Anthony?" he said firmly. "I don't know what else to say. You *may* be allowed to live." Here he laughed a little. "If they think you have potential, but I wouldn't count on it. Alexander's father is pretty pissed at you," he smirked.

To this, the golden one laughed again. "All of you get some clothes on. You are to come with us. If you resist, you'll be killed right now. Your choice."

He turned and strode out with complete indifference as to our choice. We dressed under the gaze of the armed soldiers. My heart fell to the bottom of my body, it was hard to swallow. Holy fuck...and as if it couldn't get worse, they handcuffed us. Then they escorted us to a blacked-out SUV.

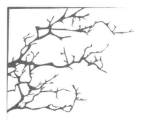

Infernum

Anthony

WE ARRIVED AT A LARGE Victorian asylum and escorted down into cellars. We were told nothing more, separated and locked in cells.

My despondency grew and I lay there not caring whether I lived or died, growing weaker and weaker. Minutes turned to hours. Hours turned to days and then I lost count. My head was dizzy and my body craved blood. My hunger was so intense that I drank from my own wrist. My once acute vision became blurry and the screams from the adjoining cells pounded into my brain, driving me crazy.

Fear seeped its way into me, overriding my despondent state. I drifted in and out of consciousness, found myself shaking with hunger, and terror more intense than I could hold as a human. My mind was cracking up and I tried desperately to gain a glimpse out of the tiny window high up on the wall. It was barred and there was no glass. We are strong to be sure, but not strong enough to break iron bars, especially in a weakened state.

In my cell, there was a metal bed, a metal sink, a toilet, and that was all. No one came. No guards, no staff, just total isolation. The quarantine was so hard to bear. Nothingness. Aloneness. My mind started to play tricks on me and I imagined Rachel there, with her warm smile and her arms open, ready to love me. Love. How I missed my beloved. I had lived and died an age since the time I dreamt or imagined—I don't know which—that Nathaniel was there sitting in my cell, so casually chatting to me. I knew I needed to do something to stop the insanity. But the screams, the cries were horrifying, agonising. Shapes in the moonlight of the cell came alive like shadowy nightmares threatening me, sending me shivering, cowering in fear. A dark ominous presence surrounded me there that chilled me to the bone. Something ancient, malevolent, and cold drawing nearer. I was losing myself, losing my mind.

I tried to cling to that feeling of love I had lost. Of Rachel. I had had a glimmer of that with Sigurd, but I had been so absorbed in my own wonder, own desires that I had forgotten love. My baser instincts had driven me to this state. This empty state.

I stood my bed upright against the cell wall and could just peer through the window. Elation filled me just to feel that cool breeze sweep over me and the sweet-smelling air. *I just need this, I just need this.*

Finally, I heard the rattle of keys and Alexander entered. His face was like the mask of death and he looked so calm that my gut wrenched inside. I fell down from my window view and hunched between the bed and the wall. His strength was ten times mine, *old blood*. Fear rushed through me like a hurricane and I cowered beside my upturned bed. I thought I had left him for dead. Faster and faster my heart sped up and I found myself shaking, almost convulsing, gasping for air.

Where's Nathaniel? I thought frantically in my petrified mind. Yet, after some seconds an unnerving calm washed over me. It was almost like being under a hypnotic spell and though fear seeped through every pore of my body, I felt oddly calm. I knew I would die now. I think I had resigned myself to it.

He stood there staring at me, holding my gaze with his dead eyes not moving, not breathing.

At length, I had to ask him the question, the question that had burned inside me for so long... "Why did your blood make me sick?"

His contempt cut through me and he said, "Why the fuck should I tell you?" he shouted, his face crumpled up in anger. Grabbing me roughly and putting my wrists in chains, he dragged me out of the cell along the dark corridor. As he hauled me, I saw what lay in the other cells, and I wish that I hadn't. Pulling me by my chained wrists, dragging along the floor, up steps where I bounded and broke against the cold stone along to a large surgical-looking room where he threw me down and left me.

Looking around, I tried to see a way out. If I could just start a fire, but with what? My hands were cuffed. And now the dread and darkness deepened. Death didn't scare me. But what preceded it did.

Alexander returned with a malevolent grin on his face, accompanied by vampires in white coats. Stern expressions, small black eyes and pierced lips gave the illusion of clones. Their close-cropped hair, an air of obedience. Empathy and individuality was lost on them and to look at them was to see total submission to their superior.

I was grabbed and led to a table. He strapped down my legs, unchained my wrists then strapped down my arms.

I didn't bother to speak, I knew it was pointless. No, not because it was pointless. Because I was terrified. As a human, I had known pain, ironically now immortal and again in a situation where my immortality was to be used against me to inflict a lifetime of suffering.

I knew I was powerless to do anything about my predicament, so meekly I just went along with it. I closed my eyes and the bloody tears on my face betrayed me. My death would be drawn out. After that, oh sweet release from this Hell I was living.

Alexander seemed annoyed at my lack of fighting, but continued in anger, his temper taken out on his obedient staff. They all worked without talking, just gazes and nods to one another. One of them, a large man, but not a vampire, came over with a needle and plunged it into my arm.

I screamed. Whatever it was burned through my blood stream like a wildfire.

Alexander bent over my face and whispered, "You want my blood, underdog? You think you are capable of taking blood so pure, so powerful?" He moved away and spoke loudly to the others, "Hmm, what first? I had thought organ donation, but that involves killing him and I want him alive. I want him alive for a long, long time."

"We could remove the lesser organs, then bury him alive?" one of them suggested.

"Excellent," he retorted sharply, his voice almost shrill. He was excited by this. He spoke directly then to me, "I've never done surgery before, Anthony, you're my *first*. I'm very thrilled." Alexander sounded demented, frenzied. The staff looked anxious, unsure, scared.

"Let us take a kidney I think."

I struggled. I couldn't believe it. I started to scream so they stuffed some bandage in my mouth whilst Alexander removed my clothes to get at my torso.

He traced his scalpel along my stomach and quietly whispered, "Remember that night in the cellar, Anthony? You were quite good. I wanted to cut you then. I wanted to bask in your blood, did you know that? Your skin is so soft." He ran his hand over my chest. I tried to stay strong, not to shudder, because I knew that would thrill him more. "I would have let you live. Can you believe that?" he asked alarmingly.

One of his people offered him a surgical swab for the procedure. "No, I don't think we need to worry about that, do you, Anthony? After all, we haven't even sedated him."

I was struggling on the table and he peered over at me grinning. "Yes, keep struggling, Anthony, it will make it more fun when I cut you open." He stepped back and started laughing hysterically.

After a few minutes, he contained himself and before I knew it he had cut my skin deeply with the scalpel. It was so fast, so sharp, it took my breath away and I gulped for air. Sweat poured off my skin, my heart pounding fast, and I struggled to yell through the cloth they had shoved in my mouth. "You demented bastard!" was all I could strain to say.

"Don't worry, Anthony, you have two kidneys, right? And let's face it, you really don't need them now, do you? Not now you are *a vampire*, yes? Well, actually God only knows, but we'll find out anyhow." He laughed hysterically.

"Alexander, what the hell are you doing?" Nathaniel boomed and strode across the room so fast, knocking Alexander across to the other side of it. "What the hell is this? I told your father he's not to be killed!"

"By whose orders?" Alexander screamed, standing up, trying to maintain some grace, some dignity.

"By my orders, you stupid grunt." Nathaniel hit him across the room again, this time harder. "Do I have to call the guards?"

"My father will hear of this, freak," Alexander yelled.

"That's right, boy, run along, run to daddy."

I was in a panic as blood literally gushed out of me.

"Stop his bleeding, fools!" Nathaniel screamed at the staff who then busied themselves around me. "You!" Nathaniel bellowed at one of the surgical staff, "give him a sedative now!"

As the nurse sank the needle into my arm and with more care, I may add, Nathaniel bent over me, his face close to mine. "Well, I think we can consider your punishment completed. You'll be safe now, hang in there." He turned around to the other staff and commanded, "Well, someone clean that and stitch him closed."

Then I felt the sedative course through my veins and I felt drowsy, very drowsy.

"Alexander injected his blood into him, didn't he?" Nathaniel asked the submissive staff. A nod. "Prepare him for gene therapy. I am to be the donor."

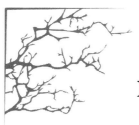

Redeemed

Anthony

SOFT SHEETS AND WARM bedding caressed my skin, and slowly opening my eyes I noticed vitality and strength oozed through my body and a serene state encompassed my mind. Stretching lazily, I looked about me, a room lushly furnished and a sweet-smelling breeze from an open window. I could sense him before I saw him, and I knew that he knew I could sense him. I could hear his heart pumping, I could *feel* it. It was almost as if I was part of him. Both distorting and comforting at the same time.

He sat there watching me, as still as stone and there were no words needed. I knew what he knew; I sensed what he sensed, even though at first, I did not know this to be true, I felt it in my gut. In my heart and in my soul.

I could see what has always been there, but which my eyes had not seen before.

Energy flashing around, faint wisps of mists. Ultraviolet light speckled in the dust of the room caught on the fading rays of sunlight, skipped around like dancers on a stage. Different wavelengths, though I didn't know what they were. I could hear the breathing of humans far away, of hearts beating, blood pumping. I swayed on the bed a little, all the senses overwhelming and Nathaniel leapt up quietly and caught me.

I stared silently at him in the wonder of my new sensations. So, this was how it felt with the blood of an older vampire, as you matured you became stronger. I felt safe though now. Safe and comfortable.

We sat in silence for a time. I didn't want that peace to end. I didn't want any answers. No future and no past. I just wanted this moment.

At last, I was compelled to ask him, and as I did so, my heart raced... "So, do I have your genes inside me, is that what's happened?"

Nathaniel remained inhumanly still before relaxing and sitting back. He smiled warmly, "No, not even we are that advanced, yet." Then he sat back on the bed pulling his legs up, "Do you know what it is to be a vampire, Anthony? Do you know how you are a vampire?"

He knew my answer to that so I just grinned at him. He continued,

"It is said that the first vampire was infected many thousands of years ago by an evil spirit. It is written in the most ancient of texts written by man, the Vedas of India, the ancient Sanskrit's."

I stared at him in disbelief. I had heard of the Vedas, I knew the stories. I knew vampires predate the modern myth and, in fact, are recorded in man's most ancient writings thousands of years old. I knew of what he spoke. And I knew the stories were disturbing. But Nathaniel had a sense of irony, even in this hour.

"But that is not wholly correct," he continued, smiling, "We know it began in ancient times, but it wasn't a spirit. We learned of this fairly recently. An ancient bacterium in the East tipped mountains was discovered. It had lain dormant probably for thousands of years under the ice. Until she found it. She uncovered it and was immediately infected. A new species emerged; whilst the bacteria merged and mutated, her DNA had no immunity, as it had never been encountered before.

"The bacteria were infectious and caused a mutation to her physiology. Unable to take food or water, she found herself hungry for one thing only, and that thing you already know. This was the start of the purebloods, the first."

He continued, "Over time, like any bacteria, it, too, mutated and some built up an immunity, which evidently would save them. For others, their physiology would not adapt. Think of it like those who have severe allergies to food, and if infected through blood, they die. You couldn't take Alexander's blood, your body rejected it, fought it. Even though you, too, are infected, but you have a *different* strain of the infection, of the bacterium. Now, however, you have the same strain of bacterium as me, in your blood. I am from a purer source than Tyrell, *but* I have mixed my blood with others, and ironically, have a stronger resistance. And I've passed this onto you." Clasping his hands together, he smirked, "You look a little lost. The bacterium *itself* alters our genomes. Over time, it has...changed, mutated. It is *that* which alters our physiology, just as some bacterium can cause disease in humans. You weren't compatible with Alexander's blood. You are with mine; you had drunk my blood before. It makes you think, doesn't it?" Shuffling off the bed he continued, "We can't always tolerate the blood of other vampires, and in these times, it has even been known that some vampires have gotten sick drinking blood from humans. If the human is on medication, say... We may be stronger, purer but maybe also more primitive and not accustomed with pharmacology."

He sat back down and let me digest this information. I stood slowly and walked to the window. Energy pumped through me in waves, my muscles stronger, my senses intensified.

I looked at my hands, my arms. Everything felt sturdier, keener. "So, what now?" I asked quietly.

"Well, first, dinner! Then let's have some fun. You'll be hungry. Here," he offered me his wrist, not moving from his seat.

I took his graceful wrist to my mouth. It occurred to me then that I hadn't even realised I was hungry. I bit and slowly drank. I felt heady but not in an urgent way, but in a languid sensuous way. I was beginning to see the world, to feel the world through Nathaniel's eyes and senses.

"Next," he said softly, "Next we are going to go out."

After I showered and dressed, Nathaniel having brought me some clothes, we walked outside, and for me every step, my foot touching the ground, a thrum of energy ran through my feet as if the ground was surging power into me.

I smiled with that feeling, it was tingly but my smile increased when I saw Nathaniel's car. I hadn't even known he could drive. A blacked-out Lotus, a practical but showy car it matched him perfectly. He grinned at me as he saw my response. I was so aware of all the smells, the sensations. The air seemed to breathe around me and the wind was a part of me, part of my soul. I trembled as I felt a deep connection as if I were some ancient creature having been awakened after a long, long sleep now connecting with all things. I was so overcome that I had to just stand there, taking it all in.

I turned and got slowly in the car still spellbound by nature, by the new world, which now surrounded me.

As he drove across the dark Mendip hills that night, I gazed in wonder out of the window, too awestruck to speak. The vastness of the rolling blackness, the fields, their ancient presence. He put some music on softly.

It was truly beautiful. I had to keep reminding myself that I didn't need to speak to him because he sensed my thoughts and he knew my emotions. I picked up on his elation, excitement, and serenity. The peace that was something I hadn't truly felt since I had stayed with Sigurd. It seemed to me that my life was either rushing into chaos or running away from it. I had found no balance since that fated night, which seemed so long ago now.

As he drove, I absorbed it all. There was no moon to speak of, but I could make out more shapes across the vast open flat countryside as his car sped and weaved through the country roads like a Spitfire. I could see cows and sheep in the pitch-black distance and was aware of the smaller animals in the spaces. My senses picking up foxes, owls, rabbits. Although I had experienced this before, this time the signs of life I was aware of were not in close proximity to me, they were a vast distance away. I saw them in my mind's eye when they moved. I had a sense of them. As individuals, it was spellbinding. I flicked the switch to roll the window down and allowed that sweet clean air to fill my body. I felt like a kid, looking in wonder at a new world.

Dazzlingly bright lights glared as we entered the tiny city of Bath and the scents were heavier. We parked up in the centre and I gasped at the beauty and the history of my charming city. I looked at the Georgian elegance of the buildings as if I was an awestruck tourist, not a local. The pillars on the buildings, the curvatures, tall, proud regal houses, and grand streets with ornate architecture. I lived here and yet it was as if I was seeing it for the first time.

We walked along the cobbled streets and under the grand neoclassical Pulteney Bridge to a bar—our favourite haunt. A decadent place where we can blend in easily.

Humans, they seemed luminous to me now and I was excited knowing, just knowing, remembering what Nathaniel had told me so long ago now, and a bubbling of exhilaration but as with tantra, was riding that wave oh so smoothly. Drawing out every sweet sensation.

We quickly had the interest of two women, and we charmed them effortlessly.

As I sank my teeth into her neck, every sensation she had rippled through my body. Her beating heart, straining as I drank, the heat from her body warmed into mine, and the settling of paralysis in her muscles as my venom coursed through her blood. The beauty and the horror.

I floated above myself. She looked euphoric after my lascivious passions and I felt so high and so connected. I wouldn't have comprehended this feeling of elation without Nathaniel's genes. Now I was a part of him, I had a part of him inside me and I understood him and his actions so completely.

I drank her with Nathaniel beside me with his woman. We were under the bridge not far from the bar, where we had found these women.

As I pressed into her against the moss-covered wall, its dampness and darkness added to the sordid and lewd atmosphere. The river beside us, fast, wild, its energy seeped into me as I sank myself into her. She groaned loudly as she felt me, and I lost all abandon.

A large gulp of air, pulling away, I had to stop now as her heart was slowing. I found this easier than I would have thought, but I wanted more. Slowly, I placed her against the wall, where she slouched to the ground, and I turned to Nathaniel.

He dropped his female, not always as charming as he looked, and as he turned around, I grabbed him and pushed him hard against the wall. Grabbing him fervently like some drunk, lustful teenager, I ran my hands through his hair. His long, dark hair felt silky in my hands, his skin soft and warm. I felt salacious. Scanning his face, this wild, blood crazed creature, why had he chosen me? Free from human constrictions, we are exempt from your judgement, your fears, and we are top of the food chain.

The women started to move. Taking a breath, he smiled. "We'd better get a taxi for these ladies," he uttered softly, as he arranged his clothes to look, well, normal.

I phoned for a taxi and helped the women up, hugging them and talking tenderly to them.

Nathaniel was uninterested but helped. We managed to gain their address and bundled them into their taxi with enough money to travel as far as they wished.

What they would remember I did not care. I would at least leave them with erotic memories of their fantastical night. Their night with vampires, though they did not know it.

He took my arm and I thought we would head back to his car.

"Not tonight, Anthony. I am not going back there tonight. Tonight, we'll stay at my place, come."

When Gods Meet

Jamie

HER BLOOD WAS LIKE no other and I felt truly indomitable, fascinated, alive.

One visit wasn't enough for this...woman. I knew the instant I heard her walking toward my room that something strange and powerful was coming towards me, but I was still surprised. Her force, whatever she was, was tangible.

She undressed slowly and purposefully and led me to the bed. I could not keep from staring at her and though I wanted to speak, I was utterly bewitched. Transfixed by her emerald green eyes—no whites; just green. She was the epitome of perfection. Though I did not know what she was, I knew she was neither human nor vampire. That thrilled me, at times she appeared partly diaphanous, and when she moved slowly I could see faint light streams emanating from her. My lust and my intrigue would get the better of me. But I had always known that. Maybe it was a dream, but I wasn't about to wake up.

"You fascinate me, vampire," and with that, our lips touched.

What was she? Her kisses were ardent, her skin soft and cold as she wrapped herself around me. A shock from her like a jolt of electricity jerked me back. But in an instant, I pushed up against her. *Am I dreaming? I want her...* My body ached for her. So much had happened so soon. Tingling all over, I kissed her body, her neck, her limbs.

Since the change I haven't met an equal, but here is someone, or something stronger than me. And after the last two vampires, this was intense, dangerous, elevating.

Her eyes subtly changed colour as I touched her and I put my hand on her stomach, tracing down. She sighed, an ethereal haunting sound.

I want her and yet she terrifies me. But I knew I'd take her, she was offering herself to me. And so soon after...whatever the fuck it was they had done to me. My craving was insatiable. And my conscience, my conscience had changed. This confused me less than I liked.

It got stranger; when I took her, I saw her suddenly in my mind before she was this...whatever *this* was.

I saw pictures of her in my mind of her human life, thousands of years ago, and then I felt very peaceful. Completely entranced in emotions, in lust.

Holding her there and looking into her deep strange eyes, I didn't want to move. She felt so...

"So, you are the one to lead Tyrell's war?" her soft voice caressed my senses like a breeze on a warm day. Then laughing, she kissed me and I started laughing, too.

I didn't know how this would end, but there and then I didn't care. *If I die now, I would be glad that I've had this to take with me.*

She sighed and whispered, "Dear Jamie, so innocent, so easily fulfilled. You have no idea of what fate holds for you."

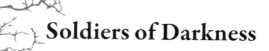

Soldiers of Darkness

Jamie

THE BATTALION WAS DISPATCHED in units of ten.

My orders were to search the city for vampires. If I thought they had potential for genetic alteration I would bring them in, sedated with the help of my soldiers. If not, kill them on sight. I was ready for this. During my time as a vampire I had met many evil bastards, killing innocent humans just to feed their hunger for blood and sex. They were remorseless, so I would be, too. And then, just when I thought my day couldn't get any better, Tyrell introduced me to my mode of transport; let's just say I was buzzing all over.

A Suzuki Hayabusa, one of the fastest motorbikes on the planet. I almost kissed Tyrell. Funny thing, I'd always wanted a motorbike, but was too scared to ride one as a mortal. My grin went from ear to ear.

Some of the soldiers travelled in SUVs, or rode Kawasaki's or the classic Ducati.

For me, dressed in black leathers, black helmet, and black visor on a black bike. The others wore various colours and had bikes of standard colours. To avoid detection, to blend in. We grouped into ten guards down to twos, threes, and fours until we would meet at our rendezvous points.

The noise of us leaving was deafening and seductive.

We were to contact each other by mobile once we arrived. Keeping off the radar was essential. Most human authorities were governed in secret by the Elite, but obviously as vampires we needed to avoid detection.

I saw Tyrell smile contentedly to himself from the window as he watched the first of his units leave the complex. Pulling on my helmet, I couldn't help but think, *and so it begins.*

Knowing that a mass of bodies would alert human authorities, the orders were to pacify these wastrels with dart guns and bring them in. If they had to be shot, their bodies would be brought back and then disposed of in the complex's old crematorium. Some of the scum would be kept alive for altering or for donor organs, some for experimentation and the rest—well, fire destroys pretty much everything.

The crematorium had been rebuilt and modernised. To avoid suspicion they had registered the asylum as a private laboratory under the guise of a leading multi-national pharmaceutical company. They did, in fact, own most of the pharmaceutical giants, so this was easy. Tyrell knew that there would be no recourse. Local government was always greedy for money and large sponsors, so he threw money and P.R. at them like pennies to the poor and the authorities sucked it up. Obediently. I learned all this after my alteration with Nathaniel, I'd found that when I concentrated I could pretty much hear any thoughts I wanted in my vicinity. It seemed everyone else was blissfully unaware of my new abilities.

For now, though, I would lead the search travelling into Bath, which is conveniently filled with alleys and cobbled back streets, the perfect hiding places for those creatures that prey on the innocent. Since my transformation from human to vampire, I had been appalled at the violence and death inflicted by other vampires. I relished the fact that I was now active in their destruction and supported Tyrell vehemently.

Tyrell had the right principles to stop the blood from spilling into the streets, as ironically now the vampires were so many, they were in danger of wiping each other out by their violent, blatant, bloody desire.

And I had been given this opportunity. I felt like a lion, the very top of the food chain. Fast, strong with the acute senses. To the normal vampire, I was like the wolf to the sheep. People seemed invisible to me now, but killing savage, ignorant vampires? Well, that made my desire burn. Deep.

I swept in and out of alleyways, throwing my bike around, revving up and generally feeling high. The first squad scoured the city. It was a weekend and the streets of Bath were busy with drunk people. Humans roaming perilously close to slaughter though they didn't know it. Lurking in the shadows close to the rabble, death waited. Patiently and quietly. I could smell it from a distance. Putrid.

Old, decrepit, sinister creatures from a twisted fairy tale, ready to pounce and devour any unsuspected victim. Their demeanour contrasted with the splendour of the elegant buildings that surrounded them. Prowling in the shadows, an old, ancient breed not unlike the tales from Eastern Europe. They didn't speak and their clothes were ragged. They reeked and they were filthy. Feeding on a man who not long before had, by all accounts been drinking and having a night out with friends. An unsuspecting victim. Only snorting noises came from them as they drank from him like eager pups feeding frantically from their mother.

My squad approached silently, eyeing the scene with disgust. But to my horror, I watched as these vile creatures began to gnaw and chew on the flesh of this hapless victim, though he was still alive. Invincibility didn't seem too grand to me now, as my stomach churned and I had to fight to stop myself being sick. A small sweat broke over me. *In God's name...*

We watched in absolute revulsion and disbelief, it was several minutes before I could signal to the others to get in place and take out these...things. Nodding, I gave the order to draw weapons, 9m semi-automatics along with dart guns strong enough to take down a rhino. I opted for the Glocks. There could be no helping these hapless fucks, the quicker we killed them, the better for society.

My second in command was Eloise, charismatic with a strength and determination that had been identified early on.

"Jamie, I've been a vampire for almost a century, but I never saw anything like this. Let's waste them." Her face showed her truth, her eyes wide with shock and her hand over her stomach as she tried not to retch. I could only nod, too shocked for words.

The disgusting vampires ignored us. Not used to having any predators, they knew no danger. A thunder of firepower and it was all over. No-one heard us, all our weapons were fitted with silencers.

The soldiers went to grab some gloves, and I wasn't about to argue with them. The corpses put in body bags, then dumped in the SUV's. The many surveillance cameras were of no importance as the Elite controlled these.

After a few minutes to catch our breath, we locked our vehicles and went off into the night to see what else we could find. My squad and I roared off on our bikes. Wheeling and revving around the cobbled streets alongside the Roman Baths and my adrenalin was coursing. I owned the city now.

We found a few others, young vampires, violent and menacing, with a quick nod to my soldiers, they were darted and carried to another SUV. Once inside, they were handcuffed, just to be sure. It was oddly quiet though, and I knew our presence in the city had been detected, I could sense others watching us from a distance. But tonight, after those cannibals I was in no mood to hunt them. They could wait until tomorrow, and both vehicles now had enough vampires, alive and dead.

As the squad drove back to command, I found myself pondering the future. Maybe it was all that killing that left me cold. I had thought I would revel in this, in wiping out those malevolent creatures. A nagging feeling persisted inside me, that this wasn't who I wanted to be. I tried to ignore it. Striding back to my bike, my legs were rigid, and I realised that my breathing was short.

My future as head of an Elite squad to wipe out the criminal scum from where? Bath, Bristol, the South West? Then what? The feeling wasn't going away.

Constrained. That was it. I was never one to follow the rules and a lifetime of obedience to my *superiors*, a killing machine—even though I believed in the cause—this wasn't for me. Not long term. They had given me a gift, and so I owed them, I guessed. But not for life.

Killing those mindless, cruel creatures had been easy. What had been harder was deciding about who should live and who would become a genetic warrior, like me. Except most of them they wouldn't be granted the same freedoms as me. They were, to put it bluntly, cannon fodder. Their identity would be stripped away, obedient slaves. Fuck, I hated servility. I didn't see the Elite as my superiors, I just saw them as vampires with the money and means to do what they chose. I understood their game plan. To them, I was the ideal candidate for the job, but I was acting. I bowed to no man, unless to save my life.

Agitation filled me and I knew my next plan was to get the hell out of here. I opened up the throttle on my bike, and let it rip as I tore through the long, dark twisted road across the murky isolation of the Mendip hills.

Previously I hadn't given much thought to my future, being too content with the blood and the attention my ego craved. But to leave the project, it would be incredibly risky to get out. I would need to keep this secret, and not even think it. If they got a hint... But getting out. The more I thought about it, the more I craved it.

My agitation grew as I neared the complex. My manner was sharp with my squad who were still busy sorting out the vampires we'd collected.

"Jamie, a good start I see. You have done well," Tyrell stated.

"Thank you, we were busy. There were some particularly obscene vampires, they were," I tried not to gag at the thought, "trying to eat their victim?"

His face showed his revulsion, brows furrowed, and his mouth hung open. "I don't think you'd want to see them, to say they stank is an understatement."

But he was also intrigued and left me to go and look for himself.

I wanted to get out of there as fast as I could, and where in the past, before my transformation I had been very gregarious, now I could act arrogant and blame it on the change. Anything to keep me apart from him and the obedient soldiers.

Eloise came up to me, "I'm surprised you didn't show Tyrell those vile creatures yourself, you're his number one." I shot her a look of indifference. "Can I help you unwind?" she moved closer, beaming at me, and holding my eye contact.

Except I didn't want her. She was as docile as the rest of them. I didn't think less of her, well maybe I did. But we were not the same and I wasn't about to waste this power bestowed on me by conforming to system for all eternity.

I had tasted Emidius. She was fantastical. Even thinking of her, I could feel her, touch her, and taste her. But there were moments when she seemed a dream, a wave washing over me. And her power, I felt aroused and knew only she would satiate my lust now. And my frustration. So, after briefing Tyrell, I grabbed my bike and headed off across the Mendip hills back towards Bath.

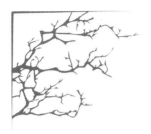

Shadows

Anthony

I TOOK A SHOWER WHILST Nathaniel slept, and I thought about my life. At every corner I seemed to be faced with some situation—fighting to survive or killing. I wanted neither. As the warm water fell over my blood-stained body, washing away my sins, I wondered, *what do I want*? There was something deeper within me, stirring. And now perhaps I had the chance to create that in my life.

It was only two in the morning so the night was still young. I wanted to explore this old city with my newfound self.

I got dressed and headed out, not even looking back at Nathaniel. He would know anyhow. I needed space from everything to explore my transformation that he'd given me.

It was cool and dark, and the antique fashioned street lamps gave the nostalgia of being in a Sherlock Holmes novel. A few people were wandering around looking for their next place to carry on drinking. I kind of missed that. Nathaniel lives in a grand part of the city and I headed off to where I still kept my flat at the other end. My muscles tightened as I realised I hadn't visited it for what seemed like ages.

Walking back, I noticed a glyph on a wall. It was drawn in red chalk on the honey stone and tiny, easy to miss. The symbol was a complete circle with a horizontal line drawn from the centre to the outside on the left. I had noticed a few of these for a while, but decided to keep the information to myself. Information was power, and I wanted to know more about this first.

Staying across the street from it, I continued but just as it was almost out of sight, I caught sight of three vampires briefly meeting by it, then moving on together. I stood still for a second. Actually, I didn't know why I did that until I found myself waiting as the cool breeze carried their scent towards me. I inhaled it in, turned around and followed their scent, keeping a wide distance.

It was fun, hunting clandestine vampires by their scent. They entered a small park just off the main street and were joined by several others. I couldn't see or hear them from where I crouched so I climbed behind a pillar on a near-by house. The golden stone scuffed my fingertips, and though coarse to touch, it was difficult to get a foot-hold. So quietly I tried, my booted feet kept slipping, and I held myself flat against the column.

From here I could see and hear a little more, but not enough. I couldn't distinguish sentences. I only caught a few words here and there. But it was exciting, intriguing and I tried to see their faces to lock them into my memory, in case I ever needed them.

They never saw me and after a few minutes of frantic talking, one of them drew the sign on the wall and then they were off and I didn't follow them. This happened within minutes. The only words I caught were gathering, Jamie and fight.

Shocked that I couldn't hear more after my transformation, they must've been whispering.

I'd keep this to myself, it could just save my immortal life.

Getting back to my flat, I had so much mail piled up that I had to shove the door open. Fortunately, I hadn't been kicked out as Nathaniel had set a number of things in place for me to cover the running of it.

It smelled musty from neglect. It's in one of the many period buildings in the city and though these do look awe-inspiring from the outside, to live in they are damp, mouldy and mostly cold due to the very high ceilings and massive rooms.

I rummaged through my stuff, put on some music, and sprawled out on my sofa. I realised I hadn't listened to music for a long time.

The music caressed my senses. I started then to remember who I was before all of this. And I had liked who I was. Nostalgia swept over me, and I craved my recent past. Before all of this sordid madness.

I sparked up a cigarette and laid there inhaling that sweet taste. This at least I could do.

The last time I had been here was with Rachel when I had fought my new instincts to drain her of blood. Before that, we had had many happy memories here. I knew then I wanted out of Tyrell's crazy programme and this *before* I was actually in it. I just wanted to be, for a while, or maybe forever. Nathaniel had told me in no uncertain terms that in saving my life, I had to join the militia. That I didn't relish. I am no soldier. I'm an artist, I used to make a living from that. Still. I supposed I had no choice for the time being, but at some near point in time, I would get away. Somehow.

So, as I lay there wrapped in my own dark world, a cold shiver blew over me, so intense that I leapt up. My temperature dropped in an instant and instinctively I rubbed my arms for warmth. *Rachel! She's in danger, something's out there.* I had to see if she was all right; I needed to do this now.

Grabbing my leather jacket, I headed out. My instinct was to go to the clubs and pubs where we used to hang out together. One of these was not far from where I lived. Although it was late, or early in the morning depending on how you looked at it, it was a Saturday so she may well be out. Saturday...I had not been aware of the concept of time or days for ages. To me, it didn't matter what day it was. A very human concept.

As I walked in there, nothing had changed. The décor, the people, and the smell of beer, all as it ever was. I hadn't been there for so long, the staff working there who'd known me well as a mortal, took a few seconds to register me. Their faces of shock told me they didn't want me there.

"Hi, Mike. I'm looking for Rachel, have you seen her?"

He frowned, his eyes narrowing beneath his shabby black hair and he avoided eye contact with me. "I haven't seen you for months! No one knew what happened to you and you two haven't been together for ages!"

His anger towards me was justified. I had kept in touch with a few people by email, but most I'd forgotten in my delirium. Rachel and I had known Mike for years and spent many evenings here, watching bands. I could understand his shock at me just turning up out of the blue. I realised then that I'd forgotten human manners.

So, I just stood there, waiting expectantly for his answer. I wasn't about to give him an explanation. Looking back, that's harsh, but it was nothing compared to the easy, simple mortal life he led. Finally, he answered.

"She was here, but she left."

"How long ago?"

"I don't know, twenty minutes. But, Anthony, she's seeing someone else. I don't think..."

"Thanks, Mike," I suddenly sensed that he fully believed I meant her harm. He sensed as Nathaniel had explained long ago, that there was something different about me. Something predatory.

It was obviously unsettling for him, having known me before I had been turned, and meeting me now. He sensed danger from me. Clever human, most don't until it's too late. I smiled, careful not to show my fangs, and I had to fight the urge to do that, and finish it with a wink. He was a nice guy and I didn't want to scare him any more than I already had.

"Mike, I know I've not been around. I had to get away, something really bad happened to me. I just want to talk to her, that's all. Just to know she's alright."

"Whatever. Don't you think you left that a bit late?"

Firmly I replied, "Like I said, I couldn't see her before. Is she with this guy now? C'mon, Mike, you know me. You know I'd never hurt her intentionally."

"I knew you, I'm not so sure now. But yeah, she's happy now. It took her months and months to get over you leaving her. Don't mess her up again. The guy, I don't know his name, I don't know him. As far as I can tell she only just met him. She seems very happy with him, not surprising."

"Why not surprising?"

"Because he's tall and good-looking. I guess that'd make most women happy."

"Still, I need to see her, to explain, to apologise. Where did they go?" I cheated here and held his gaze knowing full well that he wouldn't be able to refuse me.

"As far as I know, they went back to hers. That's all I know. You're not staying for a drink then?" he said automatically under my gaze.

"Thanks, Mike, no I'm not staying. I've given up alcohol."

Turning sharply, I was out of the door in seconds. Too fast really, but need drove me.

Rachel lived on the other side of the city so I ran towards her home. The city is tiny and it doesn't take long to cross it, even for a mortal. I stopped then and thought for a moment. *Maybe I could sense exactly where she was?* So, I focused my mind on her and just waited. I could see her, in my mind's eye.

Now I was running so fast my feet hardly touched the ground, with each step a leap, like an exaggerated sprinter. A sudden deep, intense pain hit me inside my body, making me think about the man she was with.

There was something wrong with him. He isn't human, nor vampire. He's strong, stronger than I am. I *felt* his presence. At first, I panicked thinking it could be Alexander, but no. Alexander was a vampire. What the fuck was this?

Unexpectedly I knew who it was. Gasping, a sense of relief then compounded with anxiety. And then there they were, just yards away from her home, hand in hand.

I couldn't blame her. Even had she wanted to resist him, she could not. I doubted anyone could.

"Rachel," I yelled, "Rachel." I watched them turn slowly and then the shock on her face and the sadness, the confusion.

I watched his face as he registered me, "You know this guy?" he said quickly to her.

She let go of his hand and stood there gazing at me for a few seconds longer, and then her rage bellowed out. Her face went red. Eye's suddenly small and tired looking. "Why are you here? You left me in the cold! You broke my heart!" she screamed as she ran towards me and pounded her fists on my chest.

Her anger, her tears, and her scent drove me wild. I had to fight the urge to grab her ardently and make love to her there and then. Such passion, I knew I would fight to the death for her to be mine. My eternal love.

Tears streamed down her face, her anger contorting her beauty.

"Rachel, Rachel, please. I'm so sorry, so sorry. I had to leave you, it wasn't safe, and you were not safe with me."

"Anthony, you are so full of shit. I'm safe now?" She spat the words at me. "Next, you'll tell me I'm not safe with Jamie. You piece of shit. After all those years together, you just leave. Do not touch me. It took me a long to get over you and not a fucking word from you. Don't you even dare!" she wept.

But I did grab her and pulled her against her will into me, wrapping my arms around her, basking in her scent, in her energy. She fought to get away from me, but I just held her calmly and firmly. Her strength was no match for mine.

Jamie strode quietly over, his eyes of pity. He knew why I had left. He thought for a minute... "Anthony, you should go.

She'll be alright, I give you my word," he said looking me directly in the eyes. "My *word*."

I heard his words, but I felt something else from him, it's hard to explain. I didn't trust him. Would he change her? She would become beholden to him if he did, but I had the overwhelming sense that I couldn't trust him

"No, damn you. You will leave her alone!"

He smirked, that smile of knowing that he was ten times more powerful than I was and slowly, slightly shook his head. Softly looking at me, he said again, "No, Anthony. You must go."

He reached out his hand to Rachel who pushed me away and willingly went into his arms.

In the next instant, Nathaniel was at my side. He placed his hand on my shoulder, reassuringly, "What's this? What's going on?" he asked gently.

"Who's that?" questioned Rachel.

"So, *this* is, Rachel? Good morning, my name is Nathaniel. I am a friend of Anthony's. And I know Jamie."

"You all... know each other?" she stuttered, her voice weak as she edged away from Jamie.

"Rachel, I've met Anthony once, through my job. I didn't know you and him...."

"Rachel, I have to speak with you," I interrupted. "Please hear me out. If after that you decide to never speak to me again, so be it. I won't contact you again. Ever."

She stood there, looking from me to Jamie to Nathaniel. Her mouth fell open and she shuffled back slowly. "No," she said suddenly. "No, I won't hear you. You left me, you broke my heart, shattered it into a million pieces. There is nothing you can say to me now. You could have contacted me, texted me, emailed. You didn't. Leave me now. Come on, Jamie, I'm cold and I want to go home."

"No!" I yelled and flew at Jamie. He laughed hard as I pushed him back. He whispered to me, "Anthony, you're so funny. Maybe, maybe after Rachel, I will have you, too. Or maybe all of us together? What do you say?" He sniggered.

It seemed his demeanour had changed in an instant from understanding to menace. "What do you want with her? What are you planning to do?" I yelled.

Nathaniel was by now talking and comforting Rachel, who was completely under his spell, calm and serene.

"I want her of course. I want to taste her. I want to give her the best night of her life." He stared hard, straight into my eyes.

"You'll drain her, you shit," I whispered through clenched teeth.

"Look, I have already tasted her," he said slowly. "Why not join us, Anthony? Stop acting so saintly, it's unbecoming of you. I know you screwed Josephine and Tom. And Alexander and his wenches. And now? Nathaniel. You smell of Nathaniel. Seems to me you're the one who has a hard time keeping it in his trousers," he grinned.

"Why her? Why Rachel?" I had to know.

Stepping forward away from her, he looked at Nathaniel and motioned with his eyes in her direction. Nathaniel understood and strode towards her, wrapping her attention in his esoteric charm so we could talk alone.

Whispering, he told me, "You should be grateful. Have you seen the streets out there? Before I came over to her in that sordid bar a vile, remorseless blood sucker was chatting up your ex.

I scared him off and put him on my list, I think you need to consider strongly, if she is not changed she's in danger of being drained- and not by me. That is why you must leave us."

"You're going to change her?" I gulped. I looked past him, over at her and watched as she was so easily entranced with Nathaniel. Anger swelled inside me, breathing harder trying to contain it, to stop it from exploding. But I couldn't.

I yelled in anger and grabbed at his neck, which made him laugh harder as we both knew I couldn't hurt him. Much.

"Anthony, *Anthony*," Nathaniel spoke firmly but softly. "You sure you want to do this?"

He had read my sudden impulses, my mind. A thought came so fast to save her, but...

"No, no I won't drag her into my depraved world. I will not. But you," I said to Jamie. "You cannot have her. You will not taste her blood. I left her and you know why. She means too much to me. I'm begging you."

Rachel looked on unable to speak now that Nathaniel had cast his spell over her.

"Oh, you'll beg alright, Anthony. You have no rights over her. I think we will let her decide, yes?"

"You know she'll pick you. Whatever the fuck you are."

"I'm the same as you, Anthony. And what about all those others you've had? Why, only last night?"

"Anthony," called Nathaniel again. "You don't have any claim over her now. She is gone, lost to you. I will see her home. Jamie, you find another."

"No, I don't think so, Nathaniel. I know your power, but you don't have that over me. Why don't the pair of you get lost?"

Jamie now moved to stand in front of Rachel, his warm blue eyes and wide smile dazzling and whispered, "Come, take me home."

I went to rush him and Nathaniel grabbed me. "Not now," he whispered. That godlike creature would take her, screw her, and drain her. And I was helpless to stop him. It was my fault, if I had controlled my impulses I could've saved her, made her like me and be together for all time.

"Tell him not to kill her," I said frantically. The thought of him with her made me want to retch.

"He won't *kill*, Anthony. For him, there is no point in that. And I know he's never killed a human. Ever."

That gave me some comfort. It also made me angry. I *had* killed humans, he had not. It made me angry because, in that alone, he was better than I.

The longest night. Nathaniel made me go back to my flat and stayed there with me. His presence annoyed me now. He sat quietly in the next room whilst I lay on my bed contemplating, thoughts raging through my mind.

Anger festered deep within me until at last I shot up off the bed and challenged him. "Get out, get out of my home. Your very existence enrages me!"

Calmly he got up and came to face me. "Anthony, I'm not leaving you," he spoke softly.

"Why?" I yelled at him, "You want to stop me, so he can..." I threw a punch at him. He blocked it with ease.

"I want you out, get out. I never wanted this, any of this. I hate you!" I screamed. Anger spewed out of me, raging. All this time where I had spun out of control, and the loneliness of leaving Rachel, my family, and friends. I was exploding with pent up rage, confusion, and chaos. I no longer recognised myself. I had become something that I hated, so I took it all out on Nathaniel. Because then, he was the closest friend I had.

He stood close to me trying to catch my eyes, his lips curling up faintly and his eyes luminous. He went to stroke my face, to calm me but instead, I lashed out and blocked his hand. I did not want him near me.

I lashed out again and every time he blocked me with ease. Again, and again. "Anthony, stop fighting me. You cannot win. I am your...*friend*."

"No, you don't know the meaning, you're just using me because you are lonely and afraid. Afraid of your own immortality, of eternal emptiness. That's why you didn't help me with Rachel, because you don't want her to come between me and you. But I choose her, do you understand!"

And then without thinking, I threw a punch at his face with my left fist and as he blocked this, my right fist found its way with my full force to his chest, over his heart.

He stumbled backwards, clutching where my fist had pounded his heart. He looked up at me and at that moment, I knew that he did indeed love me as a friend, unconditionally. But I could not regret what I did then, at least not at that time.

To act without thinking. My many years of studying martial arts had taught me that. To act in a way your opponent would never imagine. I would have never thought I would do that to him.

I turned and fled out of my home to find Rachel. And Jamie. Maybe he would kill me, but I was prepared to die for her, to die trying.

My anger sped me on. With Rachel, there was something else. Love; there was love. With my human friends, my human family—and it seemed the only other vampire that understood love was Sigurd; he knew what love was.

Thoughts and feelings flooded me as I raced to her home. And there I stood so soon at her front door. Listening. I could hear him inside. Hear him creeping down the stairs to outwit me at the front door. We sensed each other it seemed. There was a pause like two predators waiting to see who will act first, which one will pounce.

As he opened the door, smiling in his charismatic way, my first thoughts were *he's still dressed.*

"Of course, I'm dressed, Anthony. I only wanted to taste her. And she does taste good."

I lunged at him. "You little hypocrite," he chided. "You've drunk from loads of innocents and even killed. You've screwed your victims, you were ruthless to them. Left them scarred, battered, and bruised. Until my alteration by Tyrell, I had not."

He pushed me back with such a force that I toppled out of the door way and crashed back into the garden gate. That seemed to amuse him greatly. He strode over to me, that lean muscular creature, and offered me his hand. "Come, I know why you're here. Enough of your anger, your violence. You're too volatile. You need to control that; it really will be the death of you!" He spoke kindly.

"She's upstairs. I've explained, well, almost everything." Jamie raised his head and called past me, "Nathaniel, your progeny got the better of you, huh?" He was talking to a shadow in the distance now, and I could sense then that my saviour was indeed walking towards us. Still clutching his heart.

"Go inside, Jamie, take him with you."

I refused Jamie's hand and got up without my dignity and then ran back into her house and raced upstairs.

Rachel was sitting on her bed, bite marks on her wrist and neck. She looked languid and peaceful. Drugged from the bleeding and dazed from the bite.

"Anthony," her voice was soft and her eyes wide with the drugged venom in her veins. A delicate smile starting across her face.

"Rachel, are you alright?"

We hugged tightly and I would never let her go again. Never.

"I will do it, Anthony. You are too young, too inexperienced." And before Jamie could speak Nathaniel continued, "And so are you, Jamie. But are you sure, Anthony? Not everyone makes it through. Most do not survive. At least mortal she is alive. But the bleeding, that kiss of death, it could take her life and she will be forever lost. I don't want that for you."

"Just do it, Nathaniel," I cried without letting go of her. "And if she dies, then I die, too." Though in truth, I already had.

"What will Tyrell say, Nathaniel?" Jamie joked.

"I don't answer to your leader, Jamie. I have the authority to make or break whomever I please."

"Interesting choice of words."

I shot a look at Nathaniel. He was really pissed that I had hurt him, but he was impassioned by my act of love towards Rachel. Or so I thought. A love so strong that he himself had never known.

"I could never hurt my progeny, Jamie. I may not be *his* maker, but I have saved his life. Maybe one day you will experience that for yourself. If you live that long. Now I need some room."

And gently touching my shoulder he whispered, "Come, Anthony."

As I moved away, Rachel and I still locked eyes.

I stayed beside her, holding her hand as Nathaniel came closer. He moved towards her neck and I motioned him towards her wrist. I did not want him sucking on her beautiful neck.

Softly he said, "No, Anthony. The neck is best."

Rachel glanced at me, expecting me to say something, to do something but I did not.

And then I watched my true love die.

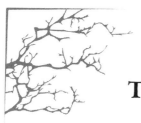

The Turning

Anthony

AT FIRST, SHE LOOKED completely dead and she nearly was. Nathaniel drained her almost to the last drop of blood. Then slowly he bit his wrist and placed it to her mouth. Nothing. She just lay there on the edge of death between the two worlds. It was surreal. I pleaded with her, I kissed her head, begged her, but nothing. She would not drink his sweet, rich blood. Nathaniel sat there patiently whilst I fumbled, implored her and Jamie stood in the doorway watching motionless, fascinated.

Still nothing. "Nathaniel!" I cried. I bit my lip, causing it to bleed. My body was stiff in anticipation.

He did not even look at me, but kept his wrist just above her mouth, blood slowly dripping in. Drop by drop. It was intensifying. Totally focused.

Then ever so slightly, she reacted. She was gradually taking in his blood.

Then a bit more dripped in, she seemed somewhat animated until at long last she started drinking from his wrist as I myself had done on so many occasions.

He took away his wrist and she lay there as still as stone.

Silence. Like an effigy she lay there, eyes closed and head tilted slightly back. Her skin turning ashen, a cold gust swept over us. I wanted to speak, but I had acted like a child enough, perched next to her, transfixed on her dead body I said nothing.

Then the convulsions started. I had a flashback to my change, gasping I looked desperately at Nathaniel but he was concentrating on Rachel. Jamie re-appeared at the door, I hadn't even noticed he'd left. He passed me a bucket and said, "You really love her? You're about to find out. Adios." He turned and was out of the door.

Rachel doubled up on her bed convulsing and I remembered what would follow. It was just the three of us now.

"Anthony, let us go to the bathroom. You know this is a disgusting experience."

I would never forgive myself if she died. She was ill, so we washed her, cleaned up and put her back into bed. I kept a cold compress on her head and Nathaniel showed his compassion by helping me clear up and nurse her. Nights turned to days and on the third night, he said, "You go out, get some air. Get yourself someone to feed on. I'll watch her."

Days followed. She had the fever, boiling hot then freezing and violently sick with diarrhoea. Seizures shook through her as her body fought Nathaniel's diseased blood. Turning vampire is a most vile and excruciating experience.

But I could not go out. I had to stay. "Nathaniel, she's getting weaker," I agonised.

"Be patient, Anthony. She is not dead, and that's the main thing now. I am feeling weaker, though. She took a lot of blood and your excellent fighting skills have left me feeling fragile. I'm not used to being the prey."

I tentatively offered him my wrist wondering if I could not sense any malevolence from him, but there was none. His eyes narrowed, he looked disgusted as he felt my fear of him. Too upset to mention it, he took my wrist and drank.

At last, on the sixth day, she started to regain some colour. Her body stopped convulsing and tranquillity sprang from her. She looked different. Her breathing had settled.

She looked almost flushed, glowing.

Her eyes opened slightly and she stared at the ceiling in shock then suddenly gasping as if she'd been holding her breath for a long time.

Looking at me, then that smile, the smile I had missed started ever so slowly to break over her face.

"My love, my lost love," I called quietly to her.

Nathaniel shuffled discreetly in his chair and sat up looking at her.

"Nathaniel, what do we do now?" I asked.

"Anthony, we wait a bit longer. You can offer her your own blood first. I will wait downstairs. Later, I'll take her out."

As she took my wrist to her mouth and drank, I had the strangest sensation. When I had met Rachel years before, I knew immediately that I wanted to spend my future with her. But I had never envisioned this. Odd, seeing my one true love draw blood from my veins.

I had opened the door to her, to step into the darkness and she obliged easily and willingly. I hoped that that was the right decision. At least she would be safe from the blood suckers roaming our tiny city.

I had thought she would resist and I would have to leave her, my heart tormented and shattered, but instead, I had her now and forever. And I had Nathaniel and my other vampire friends.

Sublime creatures of a bygone age involved in a ritual seen by the modern world as fantasy. And yet we exist, living on the edge of society, sharing blood. To be together forever, locked in love and blood.

"Anthony, can we speak now?" Nathaniel called quietly up the stairs.

I drew my wrist away from her, her dazed, dreamy face with my blood coursing through her body.

As I approached him, I saw past his calm demeanour. My own feelings of guilt and horror at my treatment towards him rushed to the fore and I was ashamed and embarrassed at my behaviour towards the one true vampire friend I had, the friend who had saved my life.

"I know how you're feeling, Anthony, I feel it. Look, I would do the same for the one I loved. If I thought you had genuine feelings of hate towards me, I would have already let you die or killed you myself.

"You will need to go back in a few days. Tyrell let you live because I demanded it but there was a price. I will return soon, I'll watch over her and guide her. I think you already know I can be trusted. We need to stay in favour with Tyrell. I have contacts, but now it is in our best interests to play it safe. I don't want to take Rachel there, at least not yet. I have already crossed Tyrell and his son for you. Don't ask me to do this again."

Nathaniel had the look of a man who regretted this situation, the timing with Rachel's transformation was not good, but I didn't want to risk her being at the mercy of any other vampire. Tyrell was right, the blood of innocents was spilling into the streets, and that needed to stop. Otherwise, we would be found out and all be killed. And I wasn't ready to die. Not now.

So, I explained to Rachel that I had to leave for a while. That there was a complex hierarchy of vampire politics, and I had to play my part in stopping the carnage. I told her Nathaniel had saved my life and I trusted him with hers, and I would return soon.

We hugged each other, not wanting to separate, but Nathaniel as ever used his charm to calm and persuade her otherwise.

"You can take my car, Anthony," he said with a mischievous grin on his face as he threw me the keys. "Treat her well," he finished.

"The same to you," I replied.

I sprinted back across the city to find his car and I have to admit, getting into his Lotus did put a smile on my face. My future, at last, looked promising.

Soldiers of Darkness
II

Anthony

"I KNOW WHAT ALEXANDER did to you, Anthony. I know." He paused as he surveyed the city before us. "You are not like them. Your malevolent companions led you astray, however fine they may seem to you. And a young vampire? Well, restraint doesn't often come easy. Still, you always had a choice and that you refused," pausing before he continued. "I'm glad you made the decision to change Rachel, and for my part I'm sorry I toyed with you. Don't forget how we first met though, you do seem to have a knack of bringing it on yourself."

Jamie was incredibly self-assured. I envied him. He seemed to have it all. He was the leader of this Elite squad that I was now assigned to, and although his past behaviour had forced my hand at changing Rachel, I had to admire him.

"You didn't behave like that?" I asked him.

"No, but my maker stuck around. And as a human, I was very conscientious about compassion. I prided myself on it. Now that has changed. After my latest *alteration* I'm fully aware I have less compassion, I'm afraid to say. A strange sensation re-

142

ally. Or rather no feeling. Back then, with my maker, it never occurred to me to take life, not even the life of a criminal. As for the sex and bloodlust, for me and my...partners, it was exciting."

He turned to face me. He had probably been just as striking as a human.

"You realised your fate early, Anthony, to exist on and on and on. Endless existence. The sensations lessen with time so you become more barbaric, more aggressive. The ones we hunt tonight, they have no such insight. They will continue to hurt or kill innocents unless we stop them. Remember that. If I see the one that was pursing Rachel, I'll let you kill him. Be assured, *that* one's intent was purely evil."

For the next few weeks, I hunted the dispossessed, those creatures that felt no remorse for their victims. Their blood spilled from my gun and washed into the gutters.

Nathaniel kept me updated, secretly by text, regarding my beloved and I missed her. I missed them both.

But night after night, blasting away the lives of those who walked the line between mindless violence and yet in some ways were not so dissimilar to me. Or at least who I had been.

Jamie and Louise were able commanders; they had the ability to brief us on our missions and to explain themselves clearly each time. The reason for our taking these lives to save the mortals and in turn save ourselves. They drummed this into us, but for me, it still seemed insane.

I left at dawn with my victims' blood splattered and soaked into my clothes, and as I stood there staring them eye-to-eye before I pulled the trigger, I felt this was wrong. It was often impossible to take that many back to the compound and Tyrell had near enough the full complement of soldiers anyway. And donors. And I reasoned with myself that taking their lives saved innocents and that they were better off dead rather than becoming those harrowing creatures locked deep within the compound cellars.

Sometimes we fed on them first before putting the bullet into their heart. Or head. Vampire or human, the body cannot function without the brain or the heart.

But one night I pulled Jamie aside, my soul tired and torn. The rising death toll was taking effect on me. And I knew I wasn't alone.

"Jamie, this is genocide. I know some of them are delinquents, like the ones that changed me. I know they have to go. But others, they are not unlike me. As I look into their eyes, I feel like I am killing myself every night. I'm just not cut out for it. I am no soldier."

Looking around us to make sure no one was listening and putting a reassuring hand on my shoulder, he whispered, "I understand, Anthony. I also feel sick of the killing, the same as you. But we are all that stands between them and society, and as much as society would hate us if they knew of our existence, I for one would rather keep the innocents safe. Pick up your gun, Anthony."

"Fuck the guns, Jamie. I need to get away."

"Not now, Anthony. Don't do this *now*. Tyrell, well, let's just say, he won't be pleased. Not now, not today. Neither Nathaniel nor I could protect you at the moment. Why not grab your bike and go for a spin? We'll be here for some time, I guess. The others are tracking our movements and after the last few weeks of Bath, Bristol, and smaller cities it seems a lot have congregated back here. Luckily for us," he muttered dryly.

I knew my insolence made him angry, I could feel it. But I was never one to obey the rules. The only thing that made me feel alive now was riding the motorbike they had issued me. And the hope of seeing Rachel.

I jumped on my bike and pulled on my helmet. Jamie had shown me how to put headphones inside my helmet, so I turned up the music full blast and revved the engine just because it quickened me.

Then I sped off to get away from the death, the blood and the darkness that strangled the life out of me.

Tyrants & Rules

Anthony

AFTER MY BLAST ON MY bike, I had joined Jamie for debriefing and then returned back to the compound with them. Jamie rode his bike, much faster than my bike, and a few others joined us as we sped the long way back across the Mendip hills, through Cheddar Gorge and into Wells. With the cool wind around me, my heart sped up and my body soaked up exhilaration, riding fast along those twisty roads, helping to clear my mind for a while at least as I threw my bike around corner after corner and raced with Jamie and some of the others. It felt like we were free, even though we were not.

On arrival, there was some commotion. It seemed Tyrell had important visitors, but no one knew who they were.

Nicolas flustered around us, catching up with Jamie.

Aside from Tyrell and his crazy son, everyone liked Nicolas. Such a timid vampire, we felt protective of him, especially Jamie. But though Jamie may not be as compassionate as he used to be, he was endearing to most and had a gregarious nature to all that he met.

"C'mon Nick," Jamie spoke informally to Nicolas who no one ever called Nick. "So, tell me, who are these guests? Surely you can tell me?"

Nicolas tried his best to politely ignore Jamie, but Jamie was persistent.

"You'll have to ask Tyrell," Nicolas told him, avoiding the question.

I returned to my quarters and sent Nathaniel a text. I needed to see Rachel. It had been weeks now.

No reply. It was too risky to call him so I made my way to Jamie's quarters. He opened the door before I knocked and beckoned me in.

"Fancy a bite?" he asked me cheekily. I noticed two vampire women sat on his bed.

Even though Jamie's face was beaming, I could see in his eyes that he was bored. They were somewhat lifeless, something seemed dead inside, his light dimmed.

Every whim and every desire provided for him, but I could see this wasn't enough. Like me, he wasn't interested. After all, when a man has everything every day it ceases to become interesting. It becomes expected, normal, and thus boring. Freedom is the only true happiness.

"I haven't seen Tom and Josephine for an age, where are they?"

"They've been held by Tyrell and Alexander. I know they'll be assigned to our squad, but..."

"But what?"

"I've said too much, Anthony. Unlike Nathaniel, I am not prepared to put myself in danger for you. You seem to demand that of others. They'll be back, quit worrying. Now, fancy a bite?"

"OK," I said dully. Though the sight of the women aroused me, I felt that it was a betrayal to Rachel, though my body did not.

"Come on, Anthony, let go a bit. I'll keep an eye on you, if you like?" He made me laugh because he winked.

"That's what worries me," I joked back. I recognised the women; they had joined our squad the week before.

I took the brunette and Jamie took the red head. They beckoned us like sirens, beautiful and deadly. I guess they thought their luck had changed, spending an evening with Jamie. How wrong they were. Had they known their true fate, they would have fought us like wild dogs.

As I plunged my fangs into her neck, she gasped and writhed around underneath me. *This is not what I wanted*. My body coursed with lust, swelling, overpowering me. She wrapped herself around me and I felt an unstoppable urge to take her. She touched me, gripped me. My mind tried to rationalise my lust as I concentrated on drawing her blood and taking her hands away and holding them down. I had enough regrets already, all too recent. Rachel was all I wanted now. For this woman, I just wanted her blood. She seemed annoyed. I can easily understand, but that was too bad. I ushered myself up from her and she lashed out, so I pushed her away.

Jamie looked on as he delicately drank from the red-head's wrist, amused by my apparent battle. It seemed he, too, was fighting the bloodlust that rages inside.

I sat there on his bed, blood dripping from my mouth, chin, and onto my chest as the brunette leapt over to me and tried to jump me. I grabbed her easily and held her down. "I don't want you. Get out."

"I'm not good enough for you? You're just using me?" she wailed. At least I think she did because by that point I had stopped listening. "Who do you think you are? You cannot just use me to quench your thirst."

Jamie by this time had got up from his woman and strode over. "Uh, yes he can. We are your superiors. Be glad we don't want to screw you. So far, I've killed every vampire I've drunk. And screwed."

Again, he gave me a sideways glance and winked, "We're simply protecting your honour," he mused.

Before she could answer, the door swung open and in sauntered Nathaniel.

"Ah, Anthony," he raised his eyebrows as he saw the two vampire women looking dishevelled on the bed, bloodied and wanting. "I see your undying love for Rachel is still alive," he said surprised.

"Nathaniel! Where's Rachel? No, I was just taking her blood. That's all."

Nathaniel looked unconvincingly at me and raised his eyebrows as if to state, *What did you expect?* "Anthony, please. Don't worry. It's not our nature to be monogamous. In fact, it is the exact opposite of our nature. In all my years, I've never come across a vampire that was. Or was able to be. Rachel awaits your presence in my room. You will find her quite changed; you should prepare for that. I suggest you clean yourself up a bit," he said and then smirked.

I saw Jamie shoot Nathaniel a look, and then I understood what he was saying between the lines.

I pushed past him and ran to his room where she sat languidly in the armchair with her feet on a table reading. Nathaniel followed slowly with Jamie behind him.

She was dressed differently, more provocatively and I could smell him on her.

"Rachel, what have you done?" I cried in a weird, high-pitched voice. "Nathaniel, I trusted you. Both of you!"

"Anthony, please! You really do have a low opinion of her and me. As I said, *and as you know,* this changes us. And I never promised anything other than to keep her safe. And I have done that, see, she is here and safe."

"Rachel," Nathaniel spoke with calm authority. "Remember what I told you? In the beginning, your bloodlust spirals out of control. Just as yours is now. Anthony remembers this. You can ask Tom and Josephine. Anthony, you should embrace this," he said artfully.

"Yeah! Well, that ended well, didn't it? I cannot believe it. This is your fault," I was talking to Jamie now and I faced him. "If you'd left her, I wouldn't have changed her and none of this would have happened."

"If I'd left her..." he started to say but then stopped. He could read the situation, I was hyped out on blood and seeing that my girlfriend had hooked up with her maker.

I watched in horror and disbelief as she got up and walked over to Nathaniel, pressed herself against him, and traced her hands through that silky dark hair, as mine had done before. They looked intensely into each other's eyes and I felt my world crumble into a thousand pieces.

"Anthony, you should know better by now than to trust a vampire," Nathaniel said suddenly.

I leapt towards him, but Jamie stopped me dead.

Nathaniel took Rachel's hand and led her off with him.

I sat on the edge of the bed the wind knocked out of me. I couldn't speak, my mouth hung open in shock like a doll.

Jamie said nothing but sat beside me. A long bleak silence draped over us.

At last, he spoke quietly, "I was only kidding about Nathaniel. I'm surprised, I guess. Look, for what it's worth, I'm sorry, man. That is just low."

"I thought we would be together, like before," I stuttered.

"Yeah, but it's not like before, is it? I mean, let's face it, you've certainly screwed around since this happened. Maybe she just wants to even up the score a little before she realises how much you mean to her. It took you a while to figure that out. The bloodlust, the sex. He is right, it's addictive. At first. At first, it's all-consuming. Just thinking about it makes me want it," he said awkwardly, and then realising what he was saying he edged a little away from me.

"Jamie, give me a break. Nathaniel gave me his blood, transferred his genes or whatever. Tom, well, you had to be there. So, they were screwing all this time. *Bastard.* He knew how much she meant to me."

"Look, you know it's different for us. Have you ever met a married vampire couple? No. For good reason. We're not great at commitment. We are too volatile."

"Just hang on in there. And that's bullshit by the way. Not trusting a vampire. I don't trust anyone here, but I'd like to. Without trust, what the hell are we? It's messed up," Jamie added.

We wandered back to his room then, and he put some music on.

I lay there smoking and trying to suppress the anger. Nathaniel had screwed my beloved. And me. Many times. At that moment I knew I'd leave this place and soon. Maybe Jamie would come, too. Get far away from this never-ending nightmare. Find somewhere without death following my every move.

"We're damned," I said at last. "Like the children of Dionysus. Damned and in Hell. Except our God offers blood, not wine."

Old Friends

Nathaniel

"NATHANIEL, IT'S BEEN an age," Sigurd bellowed out as I walked in the main room, Rachel by my side. He stood up to receive me, as was his ancient custom. Some creatures never adapt. "Tyrell has been telling me of the mission. And our young Anthony is here, is he not? I'd like to see him," he continued. I already felt bored in his presence. I had known him for a long time, unfortunately.

"Sigurd, I didn't know you knew Anthony," Tyrell added inquisitively.

"Yes, indeed. He was somewhat misguided and lost when I happened upon him. I trust he is better now?" Sigurd finished the question looking at me.

"Um, I don't think I'm the best person to ask right now. He's having a little morality crisis. That old problem of monogamy and a bad conscience that some immortals cling to at the beginning," I laughed.

Sigurd and Tyrell looked at each other knowingly. "Nathaniel, you took his woman? I didn't even think you *liked* women. Why?" Sigurd spoke sternly, standing closer to show his opposing figure and his strength.

"I don't owe you an explanation, Sigurd. You may have been fierce once, but you're pompous now. What is he to you anyway? He probably won't even be around for much longer!" I murmured back. I wasn't going to give that old phoney the courtesy of eye contact, he was one of the biggest frauds I'd known.

"What do you mean?" Rachel shrieked, letting go of my hand.

"He hurt me after everything I did for him. He can't be trusted, he's too extreme. Rachel, I didn't mean... I merely meant his anger will probably get the better of him. I wasn't implying... Rachel."

She looked at me with eyes of hate, her face hard like stone, and turned to leave. These new creatures were too volatile for my liking.

"Rachel, I wouldn't do that if I were you. I made you, you have to stay."

She didn't move and I didn't let go of her arm.

"Nathaniel, what's gotten into you? In all these years, I've never known you to behave like this!" Sigurd's voice was like white noise in my ears.

"I'm leaving," I spat. "Leaving this place. You bore me, the lot of you. Hypocrites and liars. She made me realize; I saw goodness in her. Innocence, trust. I saw it in him when I first met him, but it didn't last. Maybe that is the curse of our kind. The darkness entraps us, wraps its malevolent arms around us and all good, any good that was within us is lost. So, we turn to lust and blood to feel alive. And yes, it feels good. And every time I took her, I knew I was doing wrong. It excited me, more and more each time. Go ahead, judge me. I couldn't care less. Tyrell, maybe I will seduce Alexander next. Such a beautiful man, just to think of him."

"Enough of this insolence." Tyrell leapt up. I loved pissing him off, another pompous ass full of himself, using his title and money and claiming superiority over all others. Don't get me wrong, there were too many vampires, too many killings. But this lot...

Sigurd held him back as he leapt towards me, that made me grin. "Wait, Tyrell. I think our Nathaniel is lost and he needs *our* guidance. Guards, confine him whilst we think what we shall do with our lone wolf."

Technically, Tyrell and Sigurd had no authority over me, but something had shifted in me. Anthony's actions of malice towards me had hurt deeper than anyone here could imagine. It had opened an old wound and one which I had been covering for a hundred years. My body was heavy, as was my heart. And in truth, I did like Rachel, but she alone wasn't enough to bury the past.

"Don't take too long, Sigurd. I need to drink, bring me someone." I allowed the guards to take me to some quarters. Hopelessness filled my being along with contempt.

I saw Rachel go and knew she left to find Anthony.

Lovers Before

Anthony

RACHEL WAS WALKING down the corridor on her way to see me, I could sense her. Her heart skipping beats with anticipation and her energy tense.

As I noticed this I absorbed her energy, inhaling and exhaling slowly I soaked it up, sensing her every emotion.

Her regret, oppressive and shameful weighed her down, and as I opened the door, pre-empting her, our eyes met, that outpouring of emotion drenching itself on me.

"Come," I said quietly and led her to my room, both in silence, our footsteps loud on the tiled Victorian floor. Everything echoed in this cold, large place even though my room was lavish in that antiquated way, the place sent a chill down me. I hated it.

Out of the corner of my eye, I would catch the ghosts, poor souls no doubt who had lived here before when it was used to contain the mentally ill. Unsettling, and after my most recent change from Nathaniel, they become all the more prominent so that I had to concentrate even harder not to get distracted.

Once inside my room, I went over to the fireplace and lit a fire. Taking a deep breath, I slumped down in the large armchair, legs outstretched. The conversation I was dreading, would she now leave me for Nathaniel.

"Nathaniel's screwed us both?" I muttered and plonked myself down in the big armchair.

She sunk into the chair adjacent to me, tentatively. "Anthony, I'm sorry. He told me about you, about all the women. And the men. He said that that was the way for us, and he, he…"

"I know, Rachel. You cannot refuse Nathaniel. He *is* charming. Even I," I said awkwardly. "Look, I just want us to be together. I don't want anyone else. I can't say much here, in this place, you understand?" I waited until she nodded.

"He's possessive and I'm afraid," she added. "And that Sigurd, I don't trust him, I trust the friendly vampires least," she shuddered.

"Sigurd? He is here?" shock ran through me. I hadn't known Sigurd knew about Tyrell. I remember clearly of his warnings, but I had stupidly assumed that he was not involved.

"How do you know Sigurd?" she mumbled.

"It doesn't matter. I stayed with him for a few weeks; he kept me on the right path. No, it wasn't like that." I wanted to hold her but the thought of her and Nathaniel still made me shudder. I know I had no right to feel that way, after all I had done. But I did. But love is a powerful force. And add vampires into the mix, blood, and sex it's no surprise it gets messy. So, I fought my anger and gave in to hope instead. "Stay with me now, lay with me. Sleep in my arms?"

We climbed into bed and slept in each other's arms, as we had done before a long time ago. Before the blood.

The following evening, I awoke with my beloved in my arms. She was mine once more and this time I didn't intend to let her go. Before I got up, I heard a gentle tapping at my door and knew Jamie had come to speak.

"I'm going to need you tonight, Anthony. Sigurd has requested to see you before we leave and he wants to speak with Rachel. I think you'll find he'll keep her safe. That's my feeling anyway." Jamie still sounded empty and I was intrigued at *why* Sigurd especially requested me.

Jamie answered my thoughts, "Rumours, that's all I've heard. But the uprising, it seems is moving. I know that we need to be vigilant."

I showered, dressed, and gently woke Rachel. She looked lovely, sleepy, wrapped in the old brocade bed covers. At that moment it was like before, before when our lives were less complicated. I wanted to get her away, maybe go to Italy and find a place for us away from all this mess. Where we could spend our time in the galleries, in beauty. But I knew wherever we went the trail of blood would follow us.

I waited as she showered and once we were presentable, we made our way to the main room, where I could hear Sigurd's laugh rumble throughout the main room.

"Anthony, good to see you again. I have often wondered what you were up to. Tyrell tells me you are making good progress with the programme?" he bellowed.

"Sigurd, I, I didn't think you knew about this programme. You said..."

"A vampire never reveals all his secrets, Anthony. I knew some. But never mind that. I hope you've found your path this time? It's an honourable cause that you fight now."

"Is it?" To this remark, everyone stopped and looked at me. No-one would dare speak against it, not Jamie, not Nathaniel who now sat quietly on the far side of the room, reading a book as if everything was normal.

"What do you mean?" Tyrell spat.

"I mean the lost ones, the evil ones, as we call them. I have no problem wiping out their existence. But some of the others, it's like seeing myself die every night. Surely, we could..."

"Yes, Anthony. The business of killing is a bloody one. Don't despair. I spent a lot of my past doing that. But, you are making a difference. Fewer innocents are dying; the blood is being kept off the streets," Sigurd interrupted. Then looking to Tyrell added, "It may be time to consider a permanent force and perhaps if I may add, a reserve force. Not every man is born a soldier. I know from experience."

Tyrell was livid, but intelligent enough to know that Sigurd's suggestion made sense. His face turned from withheld anger, as Sigurd spoke and then softened some.

"I shall give this advice consideration Sigurd, we can discuss this at length later," he offered. "Now, may I introduce Jamie, the head of our Elite command force?"

Jamie played his role well. He knew enough not show that apparent boredom in his eyes and greeted Sigurd with enthusiasm. After introductions and talk of the operations, Jamie politely excused himself along with me, but not before Sigurd asked if Rachel might stay in his protective custody.

Nathaniel shuffled in his seat and watched the proceedings before him like a judge; his face wearing no expression.

Rachel, however, shifted from one foot to the other twisting her fingers together. She always did that when she was nervous.

I glanced to see Tyrell watching her before he suggested, "I think it would be better if she stayed here. There are plenty of rooms and the guards will see to her needs." His anger and impatience with such irrelevant matters was apparent. "Jamie, you are to gather the squad and head out."

IT PISSED ME OFF THAT we had to wait to be dismissed.

Jamie obeyed the order and as he nodded Alexander came swanking in.

"Sigurd," he said loudly and purposefully. "It's been too long. Father; wouldn't it be a great idea for me to take Sigurd out alongside the regiment tonight?"

"An excellent idea," Tyrell commented blandly, "But tonight. Alexander, we have other business to attend to." He motioned towards Nathaniel.

Nathaniel did not move, but stared intensely at Alexander and started to grin at him. Tyrell saw this and his jaw tightened.

"Jamie," Tyrell commanded. "Set off at once. Take this woman with you and see to it that she has some guards to attend her needs. You have more new recruits tonight, some you are familiar with. Eloise is waiting for you. I shall speak to you later. You will command Bath again tonight, for the uprising has its headquarters there. Find it and kill them all. I don't want that kind in my army." He motioned with a hand we should leave and the door was shut behind us.

My Enemy, My Friend

Anthony

IT WAS RAINING AS WE rode into Bath that evening and as we parked up, I looked around anxiously to find the newcomers Tyrell had mentioned, and before me, I saw some welcome and familiar faces.

"Tom, Josephine! I thought you were dead! What happened?"

"We had some appointments with Tyrell and his 'team'. He wanted to ensure our past behaviour remained in the past, Anthony. And you, I see. You persuaded Nathaniel to change your human woman?" he mumbled. "That's a bit stupid."

"To you maybe, but I love her."

"We know, Anthony," Josephine added, laughing, "I remember how well you loved me. And Tom. I—we look forward to meeting her." Amused, she looked at Tom. "And loving her."

"Look," I said angrily. "I did enjoy my time with you two, even though it almost got me killed. But in the end, it was empty, hollow. And I need more. And she is my 'more' so you won't go near her."

"Anthony, Anthony, calm down. We're just toying with you," Tom added. "Right now, we have to play this stupid cat and mouse game of Tyrell's. We can't afford not to tow the fucking line, most unfortunately. Otherwise, we'll probably end up as spare parts. Good for you. I hope I get an invite to the wedding, that's all I'm saying. Maybe Josephine could be a bridesmaid?"

"You're a pair of bastards," I snorted. I knew they were messing around but they'd never understand, they'd lost too much humanity over the years. Devoid of genuine feelings, of emotion. As I had thought, in the beginning, you keep your humanity, your compassion. Apart from the bloodlust that spirals out of control. But in the end, after everyone you know and love is dead, that emptiness grows, darkness consumes your heart, and you are distanced from humanity.

Humans are, after all, our food. But to be human is to love, and some achieve unconditional love. That's why the love of animals and young children lights us up, because *their* love is unconditional. But for me, for now, at least I still had some humanity. As for Jamie, he was trying to cling onto his and failing. Rachel, she had all this to come.

In that second, when I looked at Tom and Josephine, I saw Rachel and myself in the future. This is what we could become. I had to stop that somehow. Together we could stop becoming like them. I hoped.

"Anthony, come on. The sooner we can do this, the sooner we can go," Jamie called.

"I have an ominous feeling about tonight, Jamie," Eloise mumbled. "I'm going to arm up a bit more. My team will take the east side of the city and meet back in an hour."

"Sounds good. You get to take our newest members, Eloise, keep a close eye on them," Jamie warned.

"Do you think that's a good idea? I think they'd be better off under you."

"I'll second that." Josephine appeared at Jamie's side. "I'd rather be under you, Jamie."

"This is no joke, Josephine. The sooner you realise that the better. Now get yourself sorted and don't do anything until I give the order, otherwise, it will be you going back in a body bag. Understood?"

"Whatever you say."

So, they stayed with us.

We patrolled the west side of the city and sure enough, before long, I spied those strange signs written in chalk on the walls of the city. The circle with the horizontal line. They had become less frequent and maybe it was the power of suggestion, but I, too, had a menacing feeling. Again, we came across those vile creatures that had no speech.

I couldn't believe there were so many of them, where the Hell had they come from?

Like ghoulish shadows cast across a stage, even though I have encountered them many times, they still sent a chill through my flesh. Empty eyes like black pits and their stench like decaying bodies. But I suppose that is what they are. Shrouds of death lurking in the cities of men, waiting for the chance to steal the blood of the living, the last breath of their victim taken in terror.

"How can there still be more?" I asked Jamie quietly as we watched them lurking around the back streets not far from the theatre.

They seemed intent on something and at first we couldn't make out what it was. In the back streets, there are alleyways, bins, and places to hide even from our vampire vision. Then we saw it, or rather him.

A young man whose hands were tied and mouth gagged.

"He's a decoy," I said without thinking.

"What?" Jamie said without taking his eyes off the man.

"He's a decoy. It's a trap!" As I spun around a murder of vampires surrounded us and opened fire.

Instinctively I threw myself to the ground, grabbing Jamie with me. He struggled at first, not in his nature to back down.

A BLAZE OF GUNFIRE, hammering in my ears and bullets everywhere. Most lay dead, a few of our guards sent bullets off. They kept firing, and the noise was deafening.

"This is the one we want." A lean blonde vampire stood over Jamie, a semi-automatic pointing right into Jamie's face. Jamie may be god-like, but not impervious to a bullet in the head. "Take him." And then I recognised him.

"Adam? Adam, what the fu—"

"Shut up... I might have guessed, Anthony. I was told you were in on this...*plan*. Always looking out for number one. Well, you have two choices. Do I make myself clear?"

My mouth fell open and I scrunched my eyes as he was proposing to kill me, moving his gun from Jamie's head to mine. And yet I hadn't chosen this, I hadn't chosen any of it.

"You think you can join them and live? You're a stupid fuck if you think that. Take their weapons, handcuff and blindfold them, and get them back to base."

"Blindfolds won't work, we'll know where you'll take us," Jamie added strongly.

"Really, then maybe I'll shoot you here, no? Or cut out your eyes, and cut off your ears? Would that help?"

Jamie did not reply.

I saw no cuffs for Tom and Josephine. They simply, quickly exchanged glances with no expression and then we were split up. We were shoved into the back of a van, alongside the bodies of our dead comrades and taken back to their lair.

Insurrection

Anthony

THE TUNNELS UNDER THE city are prolific and the closest I ever came to something similar was when I met Sigurd. I knew roughly where they took us because the tunnels mainly occur in such proliferation in two areas of the city, but they are vast and unsafe. We were bound and blindfolded, and I was pretty sure I'd kept my bearings, at least until we got inside.

"What now, Adam?" a gentle-voice spoke to him.

"We will bargain them of course, especially this one. Jamie, Tyrell's top dog. He will be worth something, I am sure. Yes, we have seen you and your *Elite* squad blasting away the lives of our friends. You are a traitor to your own kind. And who do we have here? Anthony, you and me, on different sides. I wouldn't have thought you a killer of vampires."

I smiled and waited for Adam to approach me. "You smell good as ever. Untie me and I'll tell you how I managed to end up in this mess."

"Oh, I don't know about that, Anthony. I prefer you blindfolded and bound. You sicken me. Not long ago we shared blood and ran together on the streets. Now you are just a lap dog to Tyrell, doing his bidding in order to save your own paltry life. You are worthless to me dead. But Josephine and Tom, you did well. We have Jamie. So powerful, so beautiful. I can see why they would be protective over this specimen. Too bad we will send him back in pieces."

I could hear Jamie shuffling at the mention of being returned in pieces. But he remained silent.

"You're not going to ransom us?" I asked.

"Depends, are you worth anything to them. Anthony?"

"I'm not worth shit to them. But they have Rachel, and I will kill anyone who harms her."

"Am I supposed to know who she is?" Adam questioned.

"She'll be with Nathaniel now," Josephine added. "And you know Nathaniel. Who can resist him? But you're right, Anthony; you are worthless to the Elite, just another vampire. I heard you were not very good in the militia. Rachel was Anthony's human lover, Nathaniel turned her for him. It's all very romantic," she added sarcastically.

Adam, it seemed, ignored this information and went on, "We need Tyrell and his cronies to stop this bloodshed. We have all lost friends. You, Anthony, you were a friend once, but you switched sides."

"Tyrell won't accept any demands from you, you're too low in society, his mission is too important. If you kill us or if you don't, he will set his army on you, hunt you down and destroy you. All of you. If you cared at all, you would've stopped the blood from spilling into the streets yourselves. Don't you see, unless we stop this, we will all be slaughtered, and I for one want to live. I admit I hate the killing of my kin. Not that I feel compassion, much. But we have to cull the unwanted, the dying, and the vicious." Jamie added.

"And who are you to make such decisions?"

"I am the head of the Elite squad, chosen by Tyrell and the Elite themselves. Chosen by Emidius. I am one who had never killed before. I know who I am. Who are you?"

"I'm Adam. I am a vampire, a predator. I'm not a prestigious leader from an inbreed Elite. I am a killer and that is *my* nature. I have no inhibitions, no regrets, and until recently, no fears. I am top of the food chain and I despise all those who try to kill me for it. Would you kill a lion for hunting a deer?"

"You're not a lion; you were human with reason and intellect. Continue to kill humans and the authorities will have to act. If humans find out..."

"Humans have known for centuries, Jamie. Some know. Yes, I'll admit things have gotten out of hand, but that does not justify the genocide of all that don't fit Tyrell's ideal. And those he keeps alive are either forced to become drones in his army, like you, or are experimented on. You've seen this first hand I take it, and you think this is justice?"

Jamie fell silent. There was no doubt that the ones experimented on underwent horror on a level unprecedented by any imagination.

"So, I see. You *have* seen them and your silence tells me you don't agree. And what is done with them? Used for his purposes or cast out to live between worlds? Unable to feed on animal, plant, or human blood. We, Jamie, we have seen them."

"So, what do we do?" Jamie added coldly.

"We? So, I take it you will now switch loyalty so fast? Why?"

"Because I want my own life back. I am more than happy to wipe out those who overstep the line. But I am not happy to live my life under orders. Nobody's orders. Not Tyrell's, not Emidius. So, what's next?"

I stood there listening. I knew Jamie spoke the truth and I myself had known my days of obedience were numbered. As an artist and a vampire, I was caged in with authority. Trapped and crushed.

"We have to get Rachel out, and Nathaniel," I added.

"Nathaniel can take care of himself and if he made Rachel, I doubt he'll let her come to harm. Nathaniel is quite possessive. You haven't known him as long as we have. Trust me; he won't stick around that long."

"What about Sigurd?"

"Sigurd's there? Fuck me, that's a blast from the past. I'm surprised you've come across him. Last I heard he ate his human lover. They'd been together nearly a decade."

I was confounded at this, horrified. "You're joking right?" I wailed.

"Why would I joke? Oh…" And here Adam drew his words out to emphasise his point. "You thought he was a *good* guy."

I could hear him saunter over to me, each step against the stone floor taken slowly and deliberately, then gradually he removed my blindfold. It was dark and cold inside the cavern with only a few lanterns lighting the area we were in. Tiny flashes appeared before my eyes whilst they adjusted to the dim surroundings.

Looking me up and down with his cold dead eyes he said, "Let me tell you something, Anthony. You are way too trusting of vampires. You know the only vampire you can trust?"

I shook my head.

"A dead one. Sigurd has been fooling young vampires like you for centuries. It's almost an initiation. He's old and he can be very charismatic, but he's also deadly. Remorseless. We've all been there, and we've all learned the truth eventually."

I couldn't believe him and I certainly didn't trust him. "I stayed with him and his human lover for weeks! You're wrong. He showed me only kindness and never once did I feel any malice from him. You're the liar, Adam. Why would he show me such civility?"

"Believe what you will. He *did* eat his lover and you will find out that I am telling the truth. A few weeks may seem like a long time to you, as you're so young, but it's nothing to him. A mere blink of the eye." And his tone suggested that he hadn't realised this news was so upsetting to me. I had thought of Sigurd as a friend, as someone I could trust, rare to find. I'd thought to perhaps go back there again at some later time for solace.

"Look, I don't have the time or inclination to explain every vampire nuance to you, my innocent Anthony." As he said this he brushed his hand over my cheek and then held his hand firmly around my chin. He stared directly into my eyes. "Are you with us? This is all I need to know. But know this, if you cross me I will have your Rachel, I will make you watch as I drain her. So, don't be a stupid vampire and cross me. Decide now."

"And if I say no you will kill me now? You think Nathaniel would let you harm her?"

He smiled and stepped closer to me and whispered in my ear, "I don't think he could do a damn thing about it. He's not stronger than me. Refuse if you will, then I kill you now...my friend."

"I will join you. I hate Tyrell. And I hate his son even more. And afterwards?"

"Afterwards, we will be hunted. You will do as you will with your woman. And Nathaniel. He won't let you two go easily. Unless you find him another young innocent man, or woman," he laughed.

"And you, Jamie? I had reasoned on bargaining your life for others. What shall I do now? Why should I trust you? As you've just said, you were chosen by the Elite themselves."

"You can trust me as I now offer you my blood. It is ten times more powerful than yours, though I cannot vouch for the effect it could have on you."

"By blood? How exquisite and antiquated. My, I am shocked by an offer from one so young!"

It was at this point I thought older vampires like hearing themselves talk. I doubted we'd ever do anything other than engaging in the polite conversation where the older vampire mocks the younger vampire using words as flamboyant as possible and droning on and on about the age difference. But I thought it probably wasn't wise to point this out.

Then to my surprise, Adam said, "Now this is the plan."

Smoke and Mirrors

Anthony

THE IMPOSING BLACK iron gates opened slowly after Jamie announced us on the intercom back at the Elite's headquarters.

As we drove the old SUV in, a small sports car sped out, the driver I saw was Nathaniel and with him, Rachel. It screeched as it cut around the corner and was gone in seconds.

Jamie blurted, "That was Nathaniel and Rachel. Look, we have five minutes from the moment we leave this vehicle. You get the bikes ready. You will have to do that in three minutes. Are you ready?"

We were trying to remain composed. But in truth, we were scared. If we timed it wrong...

"Got it," I replied. "Good luck. I will find Rachel later, I can't think about them right now. At least she's with Nathaniel. Thank God they're leaving here."

The bikes were kept just alongside the entrance. My mind played tricks on me. What if he betrayed me? But I would hear his conversation as everything was to take place just inside of the main doors in the entrance of the complex. He needed that time to get out. Did he hear my thoughts? He parked up right outside and just stared out the SUV window. Then he leapt out and strode confidently through the main doors where Tyrell and his minions were waiting for him. I crept out as quietly as I could, shaking slightly. As I got the bikes ready, poised with helmets and keys, I heard Tyrell's thunderous tones.

"Jamie, what in God's name? How did you escape?" Tyrell fired questions in quick succession. Jamie paused as if nothing had happened.

"I killed them. They were easy prey, nothing more than vagabonds. I killed them all, I drank their blood, and I walked out. That is what I was designed for, wasn't it?"

I could hear shuffling and sense the unease. I wanted to turn the key. What if it didn't start...? Would they wonder why Jamie was talking so loud? No, he is acting boisterously, like them...

"Where's Alexander? I need to speak to him."

"You wish to speak to my son? Where are the others? Something's wrong if that dog Anthony isn't following you." Tyrell's voice was irritated.

"Anthony's going after Nathaniel. He's getting his bike now. We saw Nathaniel leave. When Nathaniel saw Anthony and Anthony saw Rachel, Nathaniel gave him the finger. Imbeciles. I'm tired of their games. Alexander?"

"I'm here, what do you want?"

"I was told to give you this from Tom. He said you'd know what it meant." And this was the moment when Jamie handed Alexander a small package and strolled out.

"Jamie, I require a full briefing," Tyrell shouted angrily.

"Later, Tyrell, I'm tired. I need some air." As Jamie walked through the front door, he quickened his pace and jumped on his bike.

In seconds, he and I sped off, our engines roaring.

In the moments that followed we heard Tyrell's screams, faintly as we sped away. "Get that out, it's a bomb!"

Too late old man.

We heard the first explosion, the bomb handed to Alexander.

Then the second explosion from the bomb we'd help to plant in the SUV, parked right outside the main entrance. The blast shook the main building and shrapnel flew everywhere.

In the distance, Jamie and I pulled over to watch as the main building was torn and blasted apart, the result of the dirty bomb. We watched it fall, the ground rumbling beneath our feet as the impact tore apart that Gothic monstrosity with ease.

Adam and his colleagues had gone for over kill. Ricin and explosives were no match, not even for vampires and just to be sure, we had planted a second bomb.

That was close.

"Too close," Jamie replied noticing my feelings. "I guess you want to find Nathaniel?" He sounded resigned to that fact and I didn't feel the relief I expected after blowing them all away. I knew what he was thinking because it was the same fear I had. The fear that we'd discussed with Adam and the others but they had dismissed.

The fear of the ones from the cells. The undying, neither vampire nor human. If they escaped ...well, now that was too late.

"Jamie, we have to do something. We cannot leave the people of this city to those...creatures."

"I agree with you, Anthony. But what about Nathaniel? If you don't leave now, you might never find her again. You have to make a choice. If we stay, we'll have to go back to the complex and search the outer wing where they store the weapons. Not all of Tyrell's guards will have been destroyed. We could die, horribly!" His expressions were wide and exaggerated with fear.

My eyes felt like I'd drunk four expressos. I was filled with panic.

Rachel—it made me feel sick to my stomach to leave her with him, to leave her for a second time. My soul screamed in angst over this, but I knew at my core I couldn't live with my conscience if I left innocent humans at the mercy of those things from the cells. They would escape after the blast, no doubt about it.

When I had been locked up, their screams had shaken the terror of my core. Out of control, savage brutal wights, fell creatures. They were worse than those that turned me, violent, fast, and unpredictable. They couldn't feed on man nor vampire, but it was known that they tried, having no wits about them, having lost their minds.

As I looked upon the desolation before us, I knew I would have to face those things, and risk losing her. And I didn't even trust him now to keep her alive. I had misjudged him but what the fuck, that hardly mattered now. The bleak and evil situation faced me and I faced it back, head on, not knowing if that would end my bloodied life.

Jamie stayed silent as I deliberated the choices before me. At last, I spoke, "I have a gun on me; we have the gloves and masks. They do not."

And here I paused and took a long breath. *What would happen to her if I did not leave now?* But I knew in my heart that I had to do this. Otherwise, the people here would end up ripped to pieces.

It pissed me off immensely that Adam and his cronies had decided to ignore this aspect of the destruction and leave the people at the mercy of these things. So much for his justice.

"Let's do it," I gasped out.

We hid our helmets with our bikes in the bushes at the side of the road and pulled out the face-masks we had insisted Adam give us, and the vinyl gloves. We checked our weapons were loaded. Then we made the careful descent through the surrounding fields and hedgerows towards the half-dilapidated and smoking complex.

There was no moon that night and I was glad. The huge Victorian complex was just a dark shadow from where we were and in that darkness except for the noise and the smell.

We had to act fast, we knew the human authorities would want to buzz round the complex. The Elite being so powerful and wealthy, they had always been able to keep the mortals away. Buying them off as a slack parent does to a spoilt child, but this time, they may not be so lucky.

We stuck to the hedges as we drew closer. From the distance, we saw Tyrell's minions. Some lay dead, shattered into many pieces from the dirty bombs that we had left in the SUV. Now the pandemonium we had brought right to Tyrell's doorstep spewed out into every area of the complex. It was chaotic and bloody. And it reeked.

Others were reeling in agony on the ground, doubled up from the ingestion of the poison in their stomachs. Blistered faces and some were maimed from the shrapnel. Many were severely injured with pieces of metal hanging from their faces and bodies. They hung somewhere between life and death.

And that smell, the smell of death hung heavily alongside the scent of blood. That smell that inflames my senses.

We kept to the shadows and searched for the faces of Sigurd and Tyrell, Alexander, the faces we feared to see the most. But we didn't see them. I knew Sigurd had no doubt lived, one that old. Tyrell, I was not so sure of, and his son? Well, I had been especially glad that he had personally been given the bomb full of ricin and shrapnel. He would never survive that. I did not fear Tyrell, if he lived he would obviously torture me and try to kill me, but now I had nothing left. And I would take him down with me if it came to that.

We edged closer, aiming for the wing on the south side that housed the weapons. Lots of them.

A guard stood outside the weapons vault as we approached. We ascertained immediately that he was human and as quick as that Jamie shot him. I was shocked and as he caught my glance he muttered, "He's one of them. He would've compromised us." The noise was muffled by our use of silencers and the ensuing chaos around us.

Inside another guard sorted weapons. Jamie shot him as soon as he spotted him. I stepped around the fresh corpse, the blood intoxicating me when Jamie commented, "If I'd known I would have kept him alive for you," he smirked.

I laughed quickly, almost violently for this wasn't a situation where I thought I could laugh. It was too intense, too scary and I loved him in that moment for making a joke.

"I haven't tasted blood for days. I seem to need less since Nathaniel. But I want it before we go down there. I need that."

"Then take some of mine." He grinned.

"Your blood? You would let me drink?"

"Get on with it, Anthony. Christ you're so melodramatic. Or I can grab you a stinking human if you'd prefer?"

"No, no." I shut up abruptly and there in the vault surrounded by guns, weapons, and ammunition, I took his wrist and drank. And it was ecstatic. I thought Nathaniel's blood divine but this, this was a whole new realm.

As his blood rushed through my veins, I swayed and my mind hummed. Jamie steadied me and I stood back against a wall, blood dripping from my mouth. It was like having an anaesthetic where you feel unable to do anything for a few minutes, but my senses were sharp. Burning passion, excitement ran through me.

As I looked at him a strong feeling of kinship, of belonging became tangible.

"Tyrell's," he muttered. "Come on, we got to move."

I didn't want to. I wanted to stay in that feeling, to wrap myself in it, to immerse my soul in it. How could I drink Tyrell's blood and not Alexander's? Right now, I didn't have time to question that. As I straightened myself, ready to go and grab the extra weapons, I had a flash of realisation, "We need flame throwers. They won't die with bullets alone."

"Here, take this." He threw me a sword and more surprisingly I caught it by the handle like it was the most natural thing in the world. "There are flame throwers over there. At least, I think that's what they are."

He went over to the far stonewall and strapped the device to his back. He looked like something from an action movie rather than the guy from Bath.

We had flame throwers, swords, and guns. Thank God I'd done martial arts!

"They won't be easy to kill," I suggested, strapping the flame thrower on my back.

"No, they won't, literally and consciously. But die they must. I am sick of all this shit, this mess. Let's just get on with it. And Anthony," he said sternly.

"Yes?" I answered anxiously.

"Just because I gave you my blood doesn't mean I fancy you or anything, OK?" And he grinned.

And so did I.

It's those times of high emotional stress when we need that release of laughter, it made me feel better smiling with him before I die. Somehow, it all seemed easier. I could die laughing yet.

Our backs close to the walls around the outside, in the night, looking for one of the many entrances down into the cells.

It was eerily quiet as we entered the cellar. The explosions had wiped out all the electricity, and though I could see where I was going, I could only see outlines.

Our eyesight is good, but in those dark places, even we struggle. We crept as quietly as we could, weapons poised down the steps into the basement. We could briefly make out the silhouettes of open doors.

My worse fear realised. Still no noise, just emptiness, and cold. It's strange how a place can feel so hollow, a place of evil.

A shiver ran down my spine and as it did so, Jamie reached around and touched me on the arm to alert me. Then I heard it. The sound of shallow breathing—something was down there with us, waiting.

Was it afraid? Whatever, it would try to tear us apart that much I knew for sure. We dare not talk, but we were both wondering where the rest of them were. I didn't want to think about it. In those moments a dread streamed through me, my instinct to survive sharpened. Those moments, though brief, seemed like time was ticking endlessly.

Suddenly the door behind us slammed shut and we both jumped. Now it was near impossible to see anything.

Waiting, try as we might we couldn't quiet our breathing. We heard noises, soft scuffling noises. Standing firmly with our backs to the wall as best we could with the fire canisters strapped to them, the flamethrowers in our hands, poised for any assault. I could hear my vampire heart, rich with blood pumping, *ba-bom, ba-bom* and I wondered if they could hear it, too. Certainly, they'd smell us.

Something was coming towards us, but it was impossible to tell in that pitch black where the hell it was. But it wasn't friendly; I could sense that in my gut.

"Now!" Jamie whispered to me and we both simultaneously fired the weapons.

The sudden brightness of the flames and the heat were startling and what we saw...

"What the fuck was that?" It struck me then that it had indeed been a long time since Adam's *friends* had been in the cells. I had been in them long after and though I had had glimpses, I had never actually come face to face with the experimentals.

"It used to be one of us," I muttered nervously.

"Well, it isn't now. I need light. Edge back towards the door, keep your back to the wall, and if anything gets in your way, fire," he said gently. That sounded a good plan.

Slowly I started to edge up the steps, keeping my footing. Thank fuck, I just want to get out of here. At least with some light I can see what the hell it was I'm trying to kill, or what was trying to kill me. My mind raced, and I couldn't stop seeing a picture in my mind of that *thing* after seeing that.

"Hush, Anthony," Jamie whispered.

"Ah! What the..." Something grabbed my ankle, I lost my footing and went crashing down, flames bursting suddenly, and the next thing I knew something foul was biting my neck, no, chewing my neck. Being mauled and dragged away, I couldn't reach the handle of the weapon. I wailed like a child.

"Get them off," I screamed.

It seemed like an age, but it was only seconds. Jamie had abandoned me to make for the door, which he now threw open and the light from outside, though not bright as it was still dark, seemed to flood in. I was aware then of him leaping down and kicking, with all his power, these fucked up creatures off me before setting them ablaze.

"Jesus, Anthony, this doesn't look good. I think you're...infected!" His face was contorted in disgust and fear as he stared at me and then away.

"What? Help me!"

He offered me his hand up and I staggered, holding my neck, blood trickling out.

"Give me more of your blood, it may help."

"No! If it helped, you wouldn't be infected. There's only one way I can think of that can help you. Whether or not she does is another matter. This is futile, let's get out of here."

Jamie looked repulsed at me, he didn't want to risk infection, and I couldn't blame him. It was then that I was more in awe of him. He could've left me or killed me. After all, I wasn't of great importance to him. But he chose to help me. So maybe younger vampires can pull through. The ones who still remember what it is to have humanity. Oh God, I was rambling like an Elder...

We left the burning and writhing creatures in that dark place and made our way up the steps. Their screams sounded like nothing else, high-pitched wails as if they were being dragged into the depths of Hell itself. My heart raced and my breathing heavy, I shivered violently from fear.

"Fuck, Anthony."

I was finding it hard to walk, to breathe now. "Jamie, please do something."

"Not here, I need to get you away." I knew it crossed his mind to leave me here, I could sense that. I didn't blame him. And if it wasn't for what I would become, if it was just death that waited for me, I would have happily accepted it.

Then came the voice that curdled our blood even more.

"Jamie, so good of you to come back," Tyrell called from what was left of his mouth. Jamie went white and lowered me to the floor. "Ah, I see from your expression you assumed me dead, yes? It takes more than that to kill me. I shall enjoy killing you slowly as you brought death to my son," he shouted, enraged.

He flew at Jamie, but Jamie stepped aside last minute. Jamie drew his sword and lunged towards him stopping just before he reached him. Tyrell, even more enraged now, took the bait and flew at Jamie.

Jamie ducked low and thrust the sword upwards into Tyrell's groin and abdomen and withdrew it in seconds, pulling out most of his innards with it. The once Elite vampire wailed. Jamie grabbed his hair, looked him in the eye and took off his head in an almighty swing.

"Live through that, you fucker." He dropped the head and just to be sure, booted it far away from the body.

I had no idea Jamie could fight like that. I was so mesmerised for a moment I forgot my own predicament.

"Come on sick boy, we need to find Emidius."

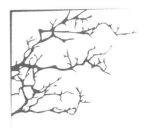

Deity

Anthony

"HOW WILL WE FIND HER and why would she help me?" I moaned to Jamie as nausea and anxiety swelled in me. Being a vampire wasn't exactly working out for me.

"I don't know, Anthony. I just *sense* that she will help. I'll find her."

We had taken a car as I was too weak for a bike. I sat there in the passenger seat once again reflecting on my changed existence. Without Rachel, truth be told, I would be glad of death, but not such a prolonged, agonising death.

"Where are we going?" I asked.

"I don't know; I'm just following my gut. Do you ever shut up? Let me think."

Then a strange sensation crept over me, like someone walking on my grave, my soul empty.

"What the fuck was *that*?" Jamie asked.

"I don't know, I just had the oddest sensation. Emptiness. Something has happened. To Nathaniel."

"What?"

"Rachel. What has happened to her if he's gone? I can always sense him since what happened at the compound. Now nothing."

"Nathaniel *went* wrong, he was one fucked-up vampire. If he has gone, that's no bad thing. It doesn't mean..."

"Spare me, Jamie. I know, but Rachel, I could sense her but less so after Nathaniel turned her, she's connected to him. If she's dead..."

"If she's dead then you'll have no more to kill. One thing at a time. You won't save her if you turn into a zombie-vampire-thing, will you? Here we are..."

He stopped the car suddenly and leaped out, and I wondered where the hell we were. In the middle of nowhere, that was for sure. The only things I could see, as the first light started to appear, was woodland.

I didn't have the energy to question Jamie. Struggling to breathe, I tried to remain calm. Strong tingling sensations consumed my body and I felt like I was morphing into something else. My skin was taut, my limbs aching, hardly moving. Barley able to move my mouth, inertia setting in.

But the fear—I would rather die than become what they had become.

I walked with Jamie aiding me like I was a soldier injured in battle, as he wrapped his arm around me to stop me from falling. I was slow and we seemed to be walking forever when we came to a rock face just outside the cluster of trees.

"This is Goblin Combe, Anthony. Just beyond there is a small opening in the rock, an entrance. We'll find Emidius there."

Taken aback that one so powerful as Emidius would be living in a cave, but then maybe she felt peace being so close to the earth. Grounded maybe, away from the human zoo. I could relate to that. Not unlike Sigurd.

Sigurd. I felt a pang of pain when I wondered about him, but my gut told me he wasn't dead. I wondered about all of the vampires I had met since my turning and how most of them had wronged me, betrayed me. I wondered why Jamie was helping now or was he, in fact, leading me to my imminent death?

I stopped. "Why, why are you helping me?" I questioned him. "Why not just kill me here?"

"The thought *had* crossed my mind," he admitted freely. "But I don't want your death on my hands, on my conscience. If you turn, I would have to kill you. I'm sick to my core of killing, it's endless. I want, no, I need something more than this piece-of-shit existence. She can offer me that, I hope."

He reminded me of a guardian angel. But definitely a fallen one and I clung to that as we walked slowly towards the cave.

Entering into the darkness through a small hidden gap, the stillness of the cool blackness surrounding me. We walked on deeper into its depths Jamie still aiding me.

I knew he was being guided there, but whether by his intuition or by her, I didn't know.

All I knew was my anxiety about the outcome was growing and he sensed that, too.

"There's a light up ahead, look." He pointed then called out softly, "Emidius, I need your help."

At first, no sound was heard and I felt another pang of panic. Could it be Sigurd or the others waiting for us?

"Ah...I only seem to get visitors when they want something. When they need my help. Even here I cannot escape."

"Emidius, you know I was fighting Tyrell's bloody war. You could have taken me with you. I'm here now. I do need you to help him, but after that, I want to stay with you," Jamie answered.

Her voice was clear and gentle with a slight accent that I could not place. "Why don't *you* help him? He has your blood has he not? And he hasn't been turned." As she finished talking she moved into the area where we stood. The pale light we saw moments earlier was emanating from her and it faintly lit the cave around us.

"Me?" he exclaimed. "I cannot do this." He carefully helped me to sit against a rock.

"I must say your compassion for this creature is intriguing. Why are you helping him?" she asked, looking from me to Jamie.

"Anthony asked me the same thing. I am sick of killing and anyway, why would I kill him? In a way, he's the only friend I have."

"Do you trust him?"

"No. *I would like to trust though.* I miss trusting. I miss feeling...something, though I almost feel nothing. Nothing but emptiness, and this sensation is growing in me. Only you can help me."

"But why would I do that, Jamie?" Her voice teased him as she walked over to inspect me as if I were some unusual object.

"You know why."

"You think you're the only vampire I've had?"

"OK. Then don't help. He'll die and it's on your conscience if you even have one, which I see you don't." He turned to leave without giving me a second look and I watched as she crouched over me, as he made his way out.

"Jamie," she called. "Come back. I will show you how to help him."

"Do it yourself," he called as he continued.

So, she did. She watched him walk away in what I thought was intrigue and disappointment. At least she let him go for now.

"So, Anthony, are you ready to become what you were born to be?" she asked me smoothly.

"And what is that? A damned creature?" I asked.

"Oh, you're not damned. Not now. And Rachel? You want to see her again. A shame Nathaniel lost his mind though. I liked him, once. But it is often the way with vampires; their minds don't cope so well with immortality."

"Do you know if Rachel's OK? I need to find her."

"But first, I need to help you. Drink from me." She offered her wrist towards me.

I was shocked, I knew she was some sort of demi-God and drinking her blood was not what I had in mind. I had heard that she *cured* Alexander and I had not heard anything about blood drinking.

"You expect another kind of magic?" her voice raised in pitch.

Captivated by her unusual eyes, so inhuman, not soulless, but definitely not human. They were incandescent.

I took her wrist to my mouth and I bit. Jamie's blood had electrified me but this, this was a potent, wild force of nature.

As I drank, it felt like a torrent swirling around inside me, a dam ready to burst. She touched my face and then ran her fingers through my messy curly hair. I felt exhilarated by her blood, her touch. She smiled and watched me with anticipation. Finally, I fell back against the rock exhausted with sensation, with intensity. I felt, I felt brazen, wild like nature herself. Like a storm gathering, like the seas crashing against the rocks, like lightning. I wanted her like I had wanted no other. Within a few minutes, my thoughts of Rachel seemed insignificant compared to the power that now raged inside me. I would take Emidius and then I would find Rachel and we would live wild and free like Gods.

Emidius laughed. "No, you will not. You shall rest here awhile, and I am not asking you. Then you will find Rachel. You may give her some of your blood, but know this, if you abuse your power I shall hunt you both and I will destroy you both."

As she finished speaking I tried to move, to confront her but I could not. "Why can't I move?"

"Because I command it. Now I have to go and get Jamie. Tyrell, Sigurd, they cannot harm you now. You will obey the law; however, you may drink from the wicked, from the deranged, from the evil, but you will *not* take from the innocent. Even those who debauch themselves; only the evil-doers. Do you understand me, Anthony? You will rarely need blood, though. Rarely."

"Am I like you?"

"No, you are not. But you have strength now unrivalled to most. Remember what I have told you. If you cross me, you shall regret it."

I nodded. She sighed heavily and drifted slowly and gracefully out of the cavern to find her vampire lover.

I sat there unable to move, knowing that soon I would find my Rachel. I felt exalted. Nathaniel was gone and my emotions swooned at his loss. But being with Rachel, just her and me, no Tyrell, no war, this seemed surreal. It was like, like the life I had before all this happened. I did not want to wait for a second longer, but conflictingly I was also content knowing that in these moments right now I had perfect balance.

I could see what was to come; I now had the strength to wield my power wisely. To keep us safe, to stay out of the circus that Tyrell had created, the politics, the games.

And as I breathed deeply and took in that intoxicating sweet earthy smell, I smiled. I felt at peace. And as soon as I felt that peace I was able to move, and so I left to find her. And I knew in my soul just where she was.

God or Immortal

Jamie

EMIDIUS PISSED ME OFF. Of course, she was all powerful but I mistakenly thought she wasn't conceited. I was finished with that shit; this supernatural world was full of power hungry antiquated creatures who hadn't evolved with the times. At all.

"Jamie, come back. You are obstinate," She rushed in front of me, I went to keep walking but she placed her hand on my chest so lightly, I was surprised I could not move.

"I am not your toy, Emidius. I am sick of all this drama," I snapped.

"I know, but right now I have to go and clear up Tyrell's mistakes. And you can help me. Then Jamie, then I want us to be together as equals. I will show you the world, as you have never seen it. You will not need blood to sustain you, but any trace of human in your vampire self will be gone, and once gone I cannot undo it. But these things will not concern you; you will exist on a different level. Do you want to be with me?"

I knew instinctively that it was what I wanted. I hated this blood-forsaken life but fear, fear of losing my identity, though vampire and partly human held me back for a few seconds.

She sensed this and spoke gently, "Yes, fear. Fear of change. But consider what path lies before you as this. You have seen for yourself the selfish cruel ways of the vampire, however alluring they seem. In the end, they are all the children of blood, wild, crazy, and without shame. *I* at least can offer you peace. And companionship." She stepped back to wait for my answer.

I was only torn for a few minutes, after all, what choice did I have? If I stayed a vampire my life would be forever getting embroiled into petty wars. She offered me power, a different existence.

"Yes, yes, I want it." Gently she reached for my neck and bit, but I interrupted, "What's this? Blood?"

"Shhh, it's the ancient way, Jamie." With that, I allowed her to bite me and drink my blood until I was too weak to stand. She helped me to the ground as my knees gave way and her face was cold as I started slipping out of consciousness.

And I heard her whisper, "*Poor Jamie.*"

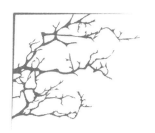

Lovers

Anthony

THE DRIVE BACK TO BATH where I knew I would find Rachel was oddly calming. I felt no haste now, knowing our future could be whatever I wanted it to be. Emidius had saved me and I would not feel the fear of the Elite or their underdogs.

Sigurd perturbed me, but not enough to break my calm mood, if he lived, which I suspected he did. *She* would deal with them as she saw fit and so I drove leisurely and serenely. And as I had expected, there on some wasteland high above Bath I drove up knowing, sensing Rachel's presence over the charred body of my psychotic vampire friend whom I had briefly loved as a brother.

Rachel, crouched on the ground beside him as his body smoked; the air thick with the smell of burnt flesh and petrol. However, his body had not burnt to a cinder. My instincts told me some devilry was afoot with Nathaniel. No body made of flesh could withstand burning from petrol and flames.

Without speaking, I wrapped my arms around her and pulled her up into me, holding her close.

She went to speak, but I shook my head, words were not important now.

I needed to get her away from here, from Bath at least for the time being. I wanted to speak to Emidius about his body, and as I stood holding Rachel close, her back to Nathaniel, I watched him, wondering why he had not burnt to a crisp.

I was so spellbound in these emotions that at first, I did not notice them, those in the tree line, shadows watching us attentively.

I did not move once I spied them, but even with the blood of Emidius, I didn't know what I was looking at. Not human, nor vampire but immortal and very, very powerful. Fear engulfed me, the hairs on my arms standing, my sixth sense kicking in. Anxiety rushed disrupting my peace, that now, I am the hunted.

"We must go, *now*," I whispered urgently and before she knew it, I had whisked her into the car and I was in the driving seat, turning the key.

The figures, whatever they were, were moving and I could sense there were many, many of them. Much more than I could see.

Then, just before I pulled away, I had one last glance in the rear-view window and amongst these things stood a mortal woman. And in my mind a name appeared, a name I did not know—Lauren.

The End.

How Can You Help?

THE MOST POTENT THING a writer can have is reviews. Without support from happy, loyal fans we fade into nothing not having the clout of the celebrity writers.

If you enjoyed this please leave a review. Some stars, a few words are all it takes. **Just three minutes of your time.**

IF YOU WANT TO JOIN my mailing list, get free stuff, join the FB group or be an ARC reader:

<u>alwaysdarkangel</u>[1]

<u>https://www.facebook.com/groups/247165435816384/</u>

---

1. http://alwaysdarkangel.com

Dark Nephilim: Book 2 Always Dark Angel

Prologue

THEY CROUCHED ON TOP of the Georgian buildings, their massive wings beating slowly. Looking down as the mortals passed unawares, these magnificent and terrifying creatures were watching, waiting. Waiting for blood; their once milky skin, now shining obsidian, crimson tinged. Red from the blood they stole, blood that they were not designed to take. Crimson that glistened under the slight moonlight in that picturesque city. Like something from a macabre Gothic tale, hair flowing in the wind and their hands gripping the ledges, their movements animalistic. But then they'd never been human.

Watching them from my hiding place, they jumped down one by one and blended effortlessly into society. Their wings remained hidden from mortal eyes by some trick, but I didn't know how. I stayed hidden otherwise they'd take my blood for sure. They'd smell it and they would bleed me dry. But not all my kin were so fortunate to escape their grasp.

These creatures were muscular, unnaturally tall with the confidence of a hundred kings. Each of them were forbidden by nature and answerable to no-one. They searched for my kind who they'd spent thousands of years killing remorselessly as they viewed us as an abomination, a plague upon the land. And now they sought us to devour our blood, our souls. It had driven them into a frenzy, the taste of blood, that swoon, hungry and savage.

These creatures changed the design of their nature from killing my kin, to feeding off of us. We, the hunters, became the hunted, and we had to hide and out-manoeuvre these dark nephilim that were once divine power, now evil.

My heart pounded at high speed and I tensed as I watched them. I wished I had my friends with me. But I was alone.

Death would fill the streets tonight. Vampire blood would be spilled as the gates of Hell had been opened. All the damned were crawling through, feasting on the souls of men and vampires and destroying their hearts.

I wanted time to heal after that genocide, after fighting in the conflict. For a while, at least I gained some kind of peace...I'd forgotten I was sleeping whilst I was dreaming; surreal images and feelings flooded my mind. But now I realised that in the realm of the supernatural, nothing rests for long...

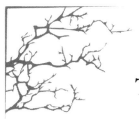

The Crypt.

Anthony

I GASPED IN SHOCK, the cold air jolting me into consciousness.

Open your eyes. Open them! But I could not. It took several pain-staking minutes, and then even longer for my vision to adjust.

As my eyes strained in that dark place, I found myself lying on an earthen floor in a dusty, mildewed crypt. I shuddered as cold from the frozen floor penetrated through my clothes into my body. My stiff frame was reluctant to move so I started by moving my hands and feet. Pain seized my body.

Short and rasping breaths, my lungs were chilled. I thought my body was stronger than this, but as my memory returned I realised I had gone to ground during autumn and it now felt like deep winter.

Ice encrusted the ivy growing over the sarcophagus in the crypt and a trickle of fear crept inside my stomach as my mind made sense of the situation that I had fled from. And now my mind pulled together the past events that had led me to hiding out here in the first place.

I remembered my not too distant past when I had been happy, mortal, and living an ordinary life. I'd had a job that I liked, and a girlfriend who loved me, introverted and introspective as I was. I glanced over to her. She looked so peaceful sleeping at my side that you could be forgiven for thinking she was dead. I'd had all the normal trappings of human existence and had been ignorantly happy.

My body jolted involuntary as the memory of the night that changed my life flooded back.

The thugs, the vampires that drained me to near death, then forced me to drink their fetid blood. They were not dashing and bold, they were vile, demonic, and without language. Their stench alone was repulsive. But my instinct, my will to survive kicked in, and I had gulped their blood fast. Things went to Hell in a matter of months.

As I lay there thinking, body rigid from the cold in that grey crumbling grave, slowly able to digest the changes that had been thrust at me. I had killed innocent humans in the beginning. My body thrust the mercy of the lashing torrent of blood lust. My soul severed from my consciousness.

Before being vampire, I wouldn't harm a thing. And the memory of that innocent woman still haunted me. Little had I known at the beginning that killing innocents was forbidden. Little had I realized that my past evils would torment me forever.

Then I'd joined with other vampires succumbing to debauchery, preying on criminals...I was an unstoppable force. The hunger drove me with an urgency that I was incapable of controlling. Then I was dragged into the crazy ideology of a despot Elite vampire war. Their mission to rid the world of the lower orders of vampires, creating an army of vampires genetically enhanced with the Elite genes to rule and govern the underworld.

I had found myself locked up, chained up, and bled and beaten before being altered further by my vampire *friend*. I was lucky to escape with my life.

As these memories streamed into my mind, my body tensed and breathing quickened. I took a slow deep breath. I was glad to have time to realise how much I'd survived and how much I'd changed.

But what am I now? A killer. A drinker of human blood. I drank the blood of a demi-god, by her choosing, to save my life. I had been infected by a creature made by the Elite. An experimental. Neither vampire nor human, he'd undergone the gene therapy to turn it into an Elite soldier. It didn't work on everyone, and those whose physiology rejected the genes were mutated into something hideous into a state of limbo, unable to take blood or food. The demi-god, Emidius, saved me with her blood after I was bitten trying to kill the crazed beasts. She told me that she saw potential in me.

What that is I have no idea, unless it is my charming personality and my extensive DVD collection. She who everyone feared, what was she really? I have no idea.

My name is Anthony and I have been a vampire for a few years and now I want nothing more than to live as I did before I was a vampire. I cannot, I know. But I want to return to life and blend effortlessly into the background. I want to live with Rachel, my lover who was turned by my vampire friend. Selfish, yes. But she came willingly, her choice made mostly by the danger of the growing amount of vampires prowling in the city.

So after all that, I went to ground with her. I had no clue actually that I could do this, it was instinct. And fear. Even though I knew I had more power than most thanks to Emidius for sharing her blood. I had wanted to get away from the fall out of the Elite's failed eugenics programme and war.

And Rachel. She thought she had killed her maker and my friend, Nathaniel. But he was old and strong and I *knew* he still lived. Though God knows how as he was doused in petrol and set on-fire after she drove a fire poker into him.

Closing my eyes for a second, I rested whilst images of that night flooded my mind with a million other thoughts. My thoughts chattered at me like birds greeting the dawn. My body started to revive and I could feel my limbs willing to be moved. Slight warmth moved gently through my body and breathing was less laboured.

Hiding in crypts in 2017. I spat a laugh at the irony of it. Who knew! And I was dressed in black. I must have been born to it!

My eyes opened slightly wider now and I looked again over at my lover. She was like an effigy, pale and cold to touch. Like death. Fitting for this timeworn place. Inside the crypt lay a few crumbling sarcophagi and frosty creepers twisted around them mixed with moss. Like something from a macabre tale.

Slowly, I sat up and felt my back ease as I moved it. I was rigid from lying still for so long and the freezing cold. Looking at my hands, they shimmered as frost had covered them and my body. On Rachel it gave the illusion of an ice queen. Gradually I stood up, blood rushing through my legs, heat reviving them.

As I stepped outside, a surge of energy rose in my body, rousing my senses. Everything was so acute—the air sweet with the scent with rotting leaves and the crisp chill of the wind on my face. Stronger than before and connected to this earth like no other. This sensation was new to me. My feet were ground to the floor as if I truly were a part of this wild nature, herself.

The cold air made my breath look like the smoke from a dragon's mouth and a small stream of light peaked through to the back of this dank place where we lay hidden, forgotten. Dreaming.

I stretched and saw that day was parting now, just as winter had left the surrounding woods bare of their thick autumn greenery. Scents and colours, warm and vivid, it was bliss.

I remembered a sensation then, such an unusual feeling as I had left Nathaniel's charred remains. The sense of being watched by something that I did not know or understand. But something that told my instincts to fear and to remember. A shiver ran over me, and I blinked quickly. Yes, something powerful and deadly. I slumped a bit at the thought. No, we would remain low key.

Nathaniel. I could feel him. I had drunk his blood. His genes had been mixed with mine. He was part of me and I knew he lived. I closed my eyes to breath in his memory, his passion for life.

Though he had terrified Rachel, wicked and evil as he is, I was excited to know he was out there. My desire to see him was strong and I found myself thinking how heartless I must be, to long for the creature who could have killed my lover. But no more, as I had more strength than him.

In the beginning, I thought of him as a friend, a confidant. And he still was in his own fiendish way. Maybe my feelings towards his friendship were in part because it was him who had saved me at the beginning of this nightmare, or at least I thought he had. Before him, I was alone and terrified with this transformation of horror, and he had befriended me. And again, when destiny led me to a fate worse than death at the hands of the Elite, it was him that saved me. I didn't trust him, but I did miss him.

A unsettling and strange power surged within me. It was a bit like wearing a new coat; I liked it but I didn't fit it yet. Cumbersome but warm.

Emidius, it was said, was thousands of years old and protective of her fragile humans. To have her blood changes you, keeps you out of reach of humanity, and I had started to sense this.

Having seen the brutality of other vampires, I was determined not to succumb to that.

Wandering back into the crypt, I took one last deep breath, trying to drive away the darkness that haunted my soul. If the Elite found me now, I'd have to face them, but I was done with this. This was not living, and living is what I wanted now more than anything.

I found myself stooping over Rachel, her pale face and pink lips, an ethereal beauty.. As I bent to kiss her a powerful yearning stirred in me. She awoke to find me drinking on her slender neck.

She sighed and I unlatched my teeth, looked at her, and grinned a bloody grin. Then I took her blood again and as my teeth sunk into her flesh, my passion awoke. As I drank from her I thought of all the people who I had bled, of my debauched past. It was as if my passion and blood lust were automated, animalistic and now I hated that. That as a vampire I cannot have one without the other. I wondered if she felt the same. Vampires, emotionally cold. Driven by sensation. It reminded me of a quote from Dorian Gray. He sought pleasure but that is not the same as happiness.

Rachel was the lover I had lived with, but she was not the same person now that she was a vampire. I listened to the pounding of her heart, and felt her emotion travel through me as her blood touched my lips, my tongue, and my throat. That incurable addiction. Blood is more intimate than sex. That sharing, the emotions and the knowledge coming from the giver, no secrets.

Covered in filth, the lust that had lain dormant came back like a force of nature.

"I love you, I missed you," I told her as I grabbed her and held her close looking into her eyes, as lovers do. Searching for something more than lust, something deeper.

That kiss was powerful, Rachel with me and our blood mixed in our bodies, we were enraptured and my previous cold thoughts evaporated in an instant.

Now I felt connected like no other. I forgot about that feeling, that emotion about *outside*, about needing to be in life. Emotion is a powerful force. So I had answered my own question. I did feel deeper, emotionally connected, but I knew not all vampires did.

She was mine and I, hers and the bond between us through blood and love felt unbreakable. Intense.

"Anthony," she whispered her voice dry. "I don't want to lose you again."

"You won't, I promise."

Maybe we had transcended from lust to something else, something stirring, something profound. I hoped so. I hoped it wasn't just *me* feeling this. Falling for an illusion like I had done, so many times before.

Love is so consuming, so erotic no words could be spoken.

That night, we made love, laughing, loving, caressing. Until now, I hadn't known that was even possible as a vampire.

For three months, we'd slept in that dark crypt, arriving in autumn, and now the signs of winter had come I couldn't even remember when I last showered. But that hardly mattered. As I let myself bond with her, nothing mattered. I'd just stay here with her and we would drink each other dry.

We lay there, like true children of the night, listening to the owls screeching and the foxes wailing in the distance. Bitter winds chilled my cold body more, but emotion inside me burned like a furnace. Nothing ventured near us and only the sounds of nature surrounded us. Dirty and dusty, we were happy.

Laying together in each other's arms, on that soil floor, watching the shadows chase across the ceiling as the light moved and bounced around I felt peaceful. If it wasn't for the hunger, I believe we could've stayed there indefinitely and just let the time of man pass us by and come out in maybe fifty years. But the hunger did start. Once awoken, it rages within our bodies like tidal waves, rushing on us and leaving us heady and dazed until we get our next fix. The blood of another vampire quickens us, but unless that vampire is powerful, it ceases to sustain us. My head spun and I felt disorientated. It was time re-join the world.

What we would find out there we could only guess, so reluctantly we left our earthy haven and made the long walk back to civilisation.

But living; life yearned for me. Gripped by anticipation to return with Emidius's blood in my veins, stronger than ever and my lover by my side. With that precious elixir my body, mind, and heart forever changed, wielding a power unmatched by my kin. I had felt that confidence growing inside me unfluctuating. Not designed for sedentary life, the mundane.

We ran mile after mile and I was determined to start over a new leaf, not to steal a life or a car this time.

"I wonder what we'll find back home, who's left. You know, Nathaniel refused to help you when you and Jamie went back to the Elite to destroy them," Rachel spluttered.

"I saw him leave with you." As I said that, her eyes widened and her mouth fell open. Before she could say any more I added, "Rachel, I had to make to make a choice. It's not because I don't care. If we didn't destroy the Elite, there would be nothing, we wouldn't be here now. Believe me, I would have rather been with you."

Pausing a moment for the words to settle I continued, "Jamie and I took a bomb, two actually, made by a resistance group. We killed Tyrell, that mad leader and his foul son, Alexander. Actually, Tyrell lived through the bombing, but Jamie cut off his head! God it was gruesome, but appropriate. Then we hunted those things, the Experimentals. I was bitten by one, we failed in killing any, and Jamie took me to Emidius. Her blood saved me. Though she was insistent that Jamie could've done that."

"What of Jamie?"

"The last I saw was Emidius looking for him. He wanted to be with her, he was sick of being a vampire, sick of taking orders from the Tyrell and killing the lesser immortals. Other than that, I don't know. I recovered, I came to find you, I sensed where you were, we went to ground. I don't know anymore."

The silence between us wasn't unsettling, it was peaceful. We ran again together. We had both changed beyond imagining from our human existence. Life would never be the same.

Eventually we arrived in Bath. As the Elite had been less interested in Rachel, I thought her home would be safer for us to stay. Her tiny Georgian terrace home on the outskirts of the city was musty and cold from the months we'd been away. Mail had piled up so we had to shove the door open. As we plugged in our phones they buzzed with missed calls, all out of date by now. After switching on the heating to get rid of the musty smell and warm up, I went upstairs in search of a much-needed shower. I had no clothes to change into so I chucked the filthy rags into the wash. We feel the cold, being sensitive to everything—noise, light and weather.

We logged onto the net to check the news to see if there were any unusual stories related to Tyrell and found a story about the complex that the Elite had used as their HQ. The building that Jamie and I had blown up. Of course, the news was false and reported the explosion due to faulty gas mains. Plausible I guess, because the site was very old. I suspect that other members of the Elite vampires gave that report to the media. I know enough to believe they have a powerful empire around the world.

I had a ton of unanswered messages and emails from family and friends. My stomach felt heavy answering these. I had to lie. I lied that I had been called away as a close friend had been ill, though I guess it wasn't so far the truth. I hated lying, especially to family and the few close friends who'd been brave enough to try and maintain contact. But what else could I do? For the time I shared with them, in their mortal existence, having to lie made the breach even wider.

I heard nothing from my vampire friends. I had expected something from Jamie. Our friendship had been short, but we had been through Hell together. I hoped he was alright. Maybe he wasn't even a vampire now.

As I wandered into the living room, Rachel blurted out, "I had a dread about the payments for my home, my bills, but it seems they're all up to date. And I just checked my bank statement and it says I'm twenty-seven thousand pounds in credit. Where the Hell did that come from?"

I knew the answer to that and I knew she'd hate it. And I had to tell her...

"When Nathaniel turned you, when he stayed with you, he set up a fund for you. You know he's wealthy, you don't know how rich he is. He made you, he saw it as his duty to protect you. Things, as you've seen, get out of hand when you enter the paranormal world and having a base, a home to flee to is important. I know you're probably pissed off about that, but really, he cared. He just wasn't stable. Something happened to him in his past that tipped his mental state. I don't know what. But anyway, that's why you're fine."

She didn't say a word. I could tell by her stern expression she was angry but at the same time, without his help, she may not have had a house to come back to. He was unbalanced, that's putting it mildly, but going from human to vampire isn't exactly the easiest trick for anyone to pull off. I would know. Any weakness seems highlighted. Any deviance becomes exaggerated.

"Any news?" I asked.

"Family, friends, work...all good stuff. Nothing macabre. Thank God."

We closed up the computers and went to get dressed. My clothes were washed and dried, though shabby from the time in the crypt. Then we were ready to head out into the city to merge into society again, and it felt odd being so completely surrounded by humans.

Even before our sleep, I had only kept the company of vampires for a long time and I had forgotten what it was like to be surrounded by mortals. Staring at them with their drinks and their carefree living, laughing, relaxing. I envied them. Life is so easy for them. They have innocence about them. They are like children, deceived, misguided and susceptible. I wanted that.

I remembered when I had thought briefly I could've been turned back to human by the Elite, and that was an interesting idea though not possible. There had been reports of the Elite's genetics plan. They were in fact breeding an army of vampires by splicing the genes from the Elite and injecting these into the lost souls they thought fit for carrying out their orders. Gene therapy not used much in human medicine and for good reason. Nathaniel had saved me, having his genes infused into me. I think that's why he has such a hold over me. I am in now part of him.

I wondered at the lengths Tyrell had gone to, to breed his Elite army of immortals before Jamie removed his head. "Ah, Jamie, I guess you're with Emidius now?" I mused.

I ran my fingers through Rachel's hair. She looked good enough to eat! We stood in a small, crowded bar, so close to humans. I loved their smell. It intoxicates me and makes me feel wild. Intentionally, I stand close, envious of their mortal existence, their life that is not driven by blood-lust. So fragile, so pure, even the nastiest humans are to me, so frail.

Sometimes a thought will rush into my mind; *I could just drag them off and drink them. But I don't.*

And so we stood there looking like them with our untouched drinks in our hands. It came to me then the reason I felt so disturbed.

I would have to teach her how to hunt. Humans. She'd only ever drank the blood of immortals so far and I don't think it had even occurred to her that she would have to drink a living human's blood. I would teach her to drink only evil doers. ·She had drunk the blood of her Maker and of me. It sustains us but we cannot thrive on it. Only human blood can do that. As she had been changed in haste during the Elite war, then captured, she hadn't spent any time with mortals. She had been held captive by Nathaniel at the Elite's complex, my being unable to be with her due to Tyrell's evil campaign. I had entrusted her safety to Nathaniel, who I had also injured, but that is another tale...

When I was first changed, I had almost bled her dry. And after her I had killed innocents. I couldn't tell Rachel this. I couldn't bear the way she would look at me if I told her that. She would see me as a heartless murderer. Which of course, I was. My first kill. I would tell her about that in time, a long, long time in the future. But for now, for tonight we would head home and I would try and put this out of my mind.

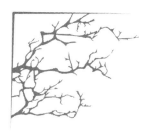

Marcus.

HIS PRESENCE WAS LIKE a nightmare. His great wings beating slowly, he was a sublime manifestation. Crouching on top of a small Georgian terraced house, near Rachel's home, he looked more animal in his stance. Not human.

His eyes followed Rachel and the slight upturn of his lips gave away his intention towards her. His thoughts seemed to muddle inside my mind and I realised he was in my head. Standing up slowly he then jumped to the ground softly, pulling in his huge black feathered wings. As he stepped towards us, instinctively my body tensed, my mouth parched whilst adrenalin pumped like wildfire.

We faced each other eye to eye, my feet planted, heart racing, and heat flushing through me. Silence echoed around us, wispy shadows flickering on buildings under the slight moon light. The only sounds our breathing.

One more step towards us and Rachel gasped, making me jump instinctively.

Lunging forward, I threw all my power at him, but he laughed and made no effort to push me aside. His expression changed when he realised he'd underestimated me and staggered back a few steps, his mouth dropping open, his arms flayed and then a huge grin appeared. He grabbed my arm, I struggled, bringing my other arm up to punch him, jerking my body back at the same time. The death grip on my arm didn't allow me to move though. I felt like a child or a fish as I wriggled from the end of the fishing line. I wasn't going anywhere. My grunted curses were cut short as the winged man spoke. I looked up to see Rachel speechless and motionless, terror etched on her beautiful face. My anger was quickly morphing into hatred as I saw her fear, but at that moment, I was powerless to do anything but listen.

"I don't want to fight you. I have come to ask for your help." His voice sounded preternaturally deep and echoed around the buildings.

In place of anger, cold fear ran through my body. My throat dry, I swallowed hard. I forced my words out of my mouth. "Leave, whatever the hell you are!" I didn't want this. The supernatural world was bigger than I could imagine and every time I went out something crept out of the shadows to bring its messed up world into mine. Or so it seemed.

Dark Nephilim: Book 2 release January 2018.

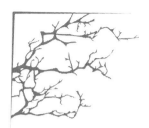

About

JN MOON IS A NEW AUTHOR who has currently written three books in her first Urban Fantasy Series. She writes Paranormal Thrillers/ Urban Fantasy.

She can be found wandering in nature, reading or upside down.

Not that she thinks she's a vampire bat, she enjoys aerial arts.

And likes hanging upside down... She's also an aficionado air guitarist.

She lives with a myriad of animals and loves nothing better than talking to like-minded souls so get in touch.

Email: alwaysdarkangel@hotmail.co.uk

Twitter: alwaysdarkangel[1]

Facebook: Moon Council of the Supernatural[2]

Web: http://alwaysdarkangel.com[3]

---

1.   https://twitter.com/alwaysdarkangel

2.   https://www.facebook.com/groups/247165435816384/?ref=bookmarks

3.   http://alwaysdarkangel.com/

Printed in Great Britain
by Amazon